Spring Heeled Jack
The Terror of London

Anonymous

TABLE OF CONTENTS

INTRODUCTORY

THERE are many theories about the nature and identity of Spring-Heeled Jack. This urban legend was very popular in its time, due to the tales of his bizarre appearance and ability to make extraordinary leaps, to the point that he became the topic of several works of fiction.

Spring-Heeled Jack was described by people who claimed to have seen him as having a terrifying and frightful appearance, with diabolical physiognomy, clawed hands, and eyes that "resembled red balls of fire". One report claimed that, beneath a black cloak, he wore a helmet and a tight-fitting white garment like an oilskin. Many stories also mention a "Devil-like" aspect. Others said he was tall and thin, with the appearance of a gentleman. Several reports mention that he could breathe out blue and white flames and that he wore sharp metallic claws at his fingertips. At least two people claimed that he was able to speak comprehensible English.

NOT surprisingly Spring Heeled Jack caused a wave of panic to spread not only across 19th century London but the whole country, the result being that any odd occurrence was quickly attributed to him, and local traditional bogey men were often eclipsed or absorbed into the new stereotype. Such a figure was bound to capture the imagination of creative artists and from as early as the 1840's he would be adopted as the subject of various gothic horror plays, and the subject of those early graphic novels called *Penny Dreadfuls*.

This would in turn shape the subsequent public perception

of Jack, and generations later ... it became quite hard to seperate the historical and fictional Jack within the cultural memory. But this was not just a secondary phenomena. As early as the initial attacks in Barnes the first Penny Dreadfuls were being published. At first consisting of popular gothic tales of murderers and highwaymen, by the time of the Spring-Heeled Jack scare was at its height they were publishing strange stories of ghosts, and even vampires, in short cliff hanger installments for a penny each. These were the cheapest publications on the market and all the rage among the enthralled populace. These undoubtedly played a role in the escalating panic and probably shaped the public perception of the phenomena. It is thus not surprising that Jack should in turn be absorbed into them. From the very beginning there was a dialectic between fiction and fact in the Spring Heeled Jack saga.

The first fictional account seems to have been as early as 1840, a play called *Spring-Heeled Jack, the Terror of London*, by John Thomas Haines, in which Jack is a dastardly villain who attacks women after he is jilted by his sweetheart. It was soon followed a few years later by the W.G. Willis play *The Curse of the Wraydons*, in which Jack is a traitor during the Napoleonic War who spies for Napoleon, and stages murderous stunts to deflect attention.

Later in the 1840s came the first Penny Dreadful to feature Jack, also entitled *Spring-Heeled Jack, the Terror of London* which appeared in weekly episodes and was written anonymously. It too made Jack a villain, and drew as much from the plays as it did reality. An earlier Penny Dreadful from 1843, *The Old Tar and the Vampire* had featured a mysterious fiend who leapt around the streets of the East End of London, and set at least one person alight with his pyromaniacal skills, but he was not overtly identified with Spring Heel Jack.

In 1863 another play, *Spring-Heel'd Jack: or, The Felon's Wrongs*, was written by Frederick Hazleton.

Between 1864 and 1867 *Spring-Heeled Jack, the Terror of London* was reissued in a rewritten version.

1878 saw the third Penny Dreadful, which appeared in 48 weekly instalments, probably written by George A. Sala or Alfred Burrage under the pseudonym of Charlton Lea. It kept the same title, but totally transformed the story. Jack is no villain in these stories; he uses his powers to right wrongs, and save the innocent from the wicked. Here he is in fact a nobleman by birth, cheated of his inheritance, and his amazing leaps are due to compressed springs in the heels of his boots. He is dressed in a skin-tight glossy red outfit, with bat's wings, a lion's mane, horns, talons, massive cloven hoofs, and a sulphurous breath, he makes spectacular leaps, easily jumping over rooftops or rivers, and is immensely strong.

In 1889 this version was reprinted, and in 1904 Charles Burrage's version was published.

Finally a remake of *The Curse of the Wraydons* was written in 1928 by surrealist Swiss author Maurice Sandoz, and later made into a film.

Jack has appeared in a variety of fictional media ever since, including an award-winning multi-part radio play, *The Strange Case of Spring Heel'd Jack*.

PART I

OUT of the enormous army of highwaymen, footpads, and housebreakers, who have made themselves famous or infamous in the annals of English crime, probably not one ever succeeded in gaining such a large amount of notoriety in so short a space of time as the subject of our present sketch, Spring-Heeled Jack.

This quickly acquired reputation was the result, probably, of the veil of mystery which shrouded the identity of the man who was known on all hands as the Terror of London.

It was at one time generally believed that Spring-Heeled Jack was no less a personage than the then Marquis of Waterford.

This, however, was distinctly proved not to be the case, although the manner of proving it does not redound to the noble marquis's credit.

That the Marquis of Waterford and Jack could not be identical is proved conclusively by the fact that the terrible apparition showed itself to many persons on the 4th, 5th, and 6th, of April, 1837.

At this time we find from an indictment which was tried at the Derby assizes on Aug. 31st, 1837, that the Marquis of Waterford, Sir F. Johnstone, Bart., the Hon. A. C. H. Villiers, and E. H. Reynard, Esq., were charged with having committed an assault on April 5th, 1837.

On that day it was proved that the defendants were at the

Croxton Park Races, about five miles from Melton Mowbray.

The whole of the four had been dining out at Melton on the evening of that day, and about two in the morning of the following day the watchmen on duty, hearing a noise, proceeded to the market place, and near Lord Rosebery's place saw several gentlemen attempting to overturn a caravan, a man being inside at the time.

The watchmen eventually succeeded in preventing this.

The marquis immediately challenged one of them to fight.

That worthy, however, having heard something about the nobleman's proficiency in the "noble art," at once declined.

On this the four swells took their departure.

Subsequently the same watchmen heard a noise in the direction of the toll bar.

They proceeded there at once, when they found that the gatekeeper had been screwed up in his house, and had been for some time calling out—

"Murder! come and release me."

The watchmen released the toll-keeper and started in pursuit of the roysterers.

When the "Charlies," as the guardians of the peace were called in those days, came up with the marquis's party for the second time, the watchman who had declined the challenge to fight observed that one of the swells carried a pot of red paint while the other carried a paint brush.

The man who had by this time grown a little more valorous, managed to wrest the paint brush from the hand of the person who held it.

But his triumph was of short duration, the four swells surrounded him, threw him on his back, stripped him, and ten minutes later the unfortunate man was painted a bright red from head to foot.

They then continued their "lark," painting the doors and windows of different houses red.

Some time later or rather earlier, Mr. Reynard was captured and put in the lock up.

The marquis and his two remaining companions succeeded in making an entrance to the constable's room.

Once there they had little difficulty in forcing him to give up his keys.

Once having obtained possession of these they had little difficulty in releasing the prisoner.

This done they bore their living trophy back to their lodgings in state, and the little town resumed its normal condition of quiet repose.

The jury found the defendants (who were all identified as having taken part in the affray) guilty of a common assault, and they were sentenced to pay a fine of £100 each, and to be imprisoned until such fine was paid.

It is hardly necessary to add that the money was at once forthcoming.

So our readers will see that this disgraceful affair proves

conclusively that the Marquis of Waterford and Spring-Heeled Jack had a separate existence, unless the marquis was gifted with the power of being in two places at once.

In the *Annual Register*, Feb. 20th, 1837, we find the following—

"OUTRAGE ON A YOUNG LADY.—Frequent representations have of late been made to the Lord Mayor, of the alarm excited by a miscreant, who haunted the lanes and lonely places in the neighbourhood of the metropolis for the purpose of terrifying women and children."

"For some time these statements were supposed to be greatly exaggerated."

"However, the matter was put beyond a doubt by the following circumstance:—"

"A Mr. Alsop, who resided in Bearbind-lane, a lonely spot between the villages of Bow and Old Ford, attended at Lambeth-street Office, with his three daughters, to state the particulars of an outrageous assault upon one of his daughters, by a fellow who goes by the name of the suburban ghost, or 'Spring-Heeled Jack.'"

"Miss Jane Alsop, one of the young ladies, gave the following evidence:—"

"About a quarter to nine o'clock on the preceding night she heard a violent ringing at the gate in front of the house; and on going to the door to see what was the matter, she saw a man standing outside, of whom she inquired what was the matter."

"The person instantly replied that he was a policeman, and said, 'For Heaven's sake bring me a light, for we have caught Spring-Heeled Jack here in the lane.'"

"She returned into the house and brought a candle and handed it to the person, who appeared enveloped in a large cloak."

"The instant she had done so, however, he threw off his outer garment, and applying the lighted candle to his breast, presented a most hideous and frightful appearance, and vomited forth a quantity of blue and white flame from his mouth, and his eyes resembled red balls of fire."

"From the hasty glance which her fright enabled her to get at his person, she observed that he wore a large helmet, and his dress, which appeared to fit him very tight, seemed to her to resemble white oilskin."

"Without uttering a sentence he darted at her, and catching her partly by her dress and the back part of her neck, placed her head under one of his arms, and commenced bearing her down with his claws, which she was certain were of some metallic substance."

"She screamed out as loud as she could for assistance, and by considerable exertion got away from him, and ran towards the house to get in."

"Her assailant, however, followed her, and caught her on the steps leading to the hall door, when he again used considerable violence, tore her neck and arms with his claws, as well as a quantity of hair from her head; but she was at length rescued from his grasp by one of her sisters."

"Miss Alsop added that she had suffered considerably all night from the shock she had sustained, and was then in extreme pain, both from the injury done to her arm, and the wounds and scratches inflicted by the miscreant on her shoulders and neck, with his claws or hands."

This story was fully confirmed by Mr. Alsop, and his other daughter said—

"That the fellow kept knocking and ringing at the gate after she had dragged her sister away from him, but scampered off when she shouted from an upper window for a policeman."

"He left his cloak behind him, which someone else picked up, and ran off with."

And again on Feb. 26th, of the same year, we find the following:—

"'THE GHOST, alias 'SPRING-HEELED JACK' AGAIN.—At Lambeth-street office, Mr. Scales, a respectable butcher, residing in Narrow-street, Limehouse, accompanied by his sister, a young woman eighteen years of age, made the following statement relative to the further gambols of Spring-Heeled Jack:—"

"Miss Scales stated that on the evening of Wednesday last, at about half-past eight o'clock, as she and her sister were returning from the house of their brother, and while passing along Green Dragon-alley, they observed some, person standing in an angle in the passage."

"She was in advance of her sister at the time, and just as she came up to the person, who was enveloped in a large cloak, he spurted a quantity of blue flame right in her face, which deprived her of her sight, and so alarmed her, that she instantly dropped to the ground, and was seized with violent fits, which continued for several hours."

"Mr. Scales said that on the evening in question, in a few minutes after his sisters had left the house, he heard the loud screams of one of them, and on running up Green Dragon-alley he found his sister Lucy, who had just given her statement, on the ground in a fit, and his other sister endeavoring to hold and support her."

"She was removed home, and he then learned from his other sister what had happened."

"She described the person to be of tall, thin, and gentlemanly appearance, enveloped in a large cloak, and carried in front of his person a small lamp, or bull's eye, similar to those in possession of the police."

"The individual did not utter a word, nor did he attempt to lay hands on them, but walked away in an instant."

"Every effort was subsequently made by the police to discover the author of these and similar outrages, and several persons were taken up and underwent lengthened examinations, but were finally set at liberty, nothing being elicited to fix the offence upon them."

Articles and paragraphs of this nature were of almost daily occurrence at this period, and the public excitement rose to such a pitch that "Vigilance Committees" were formed in various parts of London to try and put a stop to the Terror's pranks and depredations, even if they could not succeed in securing his apprehension. There could be no possible doubt that there was very little exaggeration in the extraordinary statements as to Spring-Heeled Jack's antics.

A bet of two hundred pounds, which became the talk of the clubs and coffee-houses, did more to add to Jack's reputation for supernatural powers than all the talk of mail-coach guards, market people, and servant girls.

A party of gentlemen were travelling by the then newly-opened London and North-Western Railway.

As they neared the northern end of the Primrose Hill tunnel they observed the figure of Jack sitting on a post, looking exactly as his Satanic Majesty is usually represented in picture books or on the stage.

"By Jove! there's Spring-Heeled Jack," cried Colonel Fortescue, one of the travellers.

"Yes," cried Major Howard, one of his companions, "and I'll bet you two hundred pounds even that he's at the other end of the tunnel when we arrive there."

"Done!" cried the colonel.

And sure enough as the train emerged once more into the

open air there was Spring-Heeled Jack at the side of the line, his long moustaches twirled up the sides of his prominent nose, and stream of sulphurous flame seeming to pour out from between his lips.

Another instant and he had disappeared.

The whole party in the train were almost paralysed for a time, although most of them had "set their squadron in the field," and hardly knew what fear meant.

Colonel Fortescue handed the major the two hundred pounds, and the affair became a nine-days' wonder.

The solution was, no doubt, simple enough.

Spring-Heeled Jack had sprung on to the moving train at the rear, and during its passage through the tunnel had made his way to the front, and then, with a bound, had made his appearance in front of the advancing train.

Be this as it may, the unimpeachable evidence of men of position, like the gallant officers, backed up, as it was, by the payment and receipt of the two hundred pounds, brought Jack with a bound, like one from his own spring heels, to the utmost pinnacle of notorious fame.

We have no particulars of the exact mechanism that enabled Spring-heeled Jack to make such extraordinary bounds.

To jump clear over a stage coach, with its usual complement of passengers on top, was as easy to him as stepping across a gutter would be to any ordinary man.

The secret of these boots had died with the inventor, and perhaps it is as well.

We have no doubt that if those boots were purchasable articles many of our readers would be tempted to leave off taking in *The Boy's Standard*, so as to be able to save up more pennies towards the purchase of a pair.

Fancy, if you can, what would be the consequence of a small army of Spring-heels in every district.

To return, however, to our hero.

His dress was most striking.

It consisted of a tight-fitting garment, which covered him from his neck to his feet.

This garment was of a blood-red colour.

One foot was encased in a high-heeled, pointed shoe, while the other was hidden in a peculiar affair, something like a cow's hoof, in imitation, no doubt, of the "cloven hoof" of Satan. It was generally supposed that the "springing" mechanism was contained in that hoof.

He wore a very small black cap on his head, in which was fastened one bright crimson feather.

The upper part of his face was covered with black domino.

When not in action the whole was concealed by an enormous black cloak, with one hood, and which literally covered him from head to foot.

He did not always confine himself to this dress though, for sometimes he would place the head of an animal, constructed out of paper and plaster, over his own, and make changes in his attire.

Still, the above was his favourite costume, and our readers may imagine it was a most effective one for Jack's purpose.

These are almost all the published facts about this extraordinary man.

But we have been favoured by the descendants of Spring-Heeled Jack with the perusal of his "Journal" or "Confessions," call it which you will.

The only condition imposed upon us in return for this very great favour is that we shall conceal the real name of the hero of this truly extraordinary story.

The reason for this secresy is obvious.

The descendants of Spring-Heeled Jack are at the present time large landed proprietors in South of England, and although had it not been for our hero's exploits they would not at the present time be occupying that position, still one can hardly wonder at their not wishing the real name of Spring-Heeled Jack to become known.

As it will, however, be necessary for the proper unravelling of our story that some name should be used we will bestow upon our hero the name of Dacre.

Jack Dacre was the son of a baronet whose creation went back as far back as 1619.

Jack's father had been a younger son, and, as was frequently the case in those days, he had been sent out to India to see what he could do for himself.

This was rendered necessary by the fact that I although the Dacres possessed a considerable amount of land the whole of it was strictly entailed.

This fact was added to the perhaps more important one that each individual Dacre in possession of the title and estates seemed to consider that it was his duty to live close up to his income, and to give his younger sons nothing to start in life with, save a good education.

That is to say, the younger sons had the run of the house.

They were taught to shoot by the keepers; to ride by the grooms; to throw a fly, perhaps, by the gardener; and to pick up what little "book-learning" they could.

Not altogether a bad education, perhaps, in those days when fortunes could be made in India by any who had fair connections, plenty of pluck, and plenty of industry.

Jack's father was early told that he could expect no money out of the estate, and he was also informed that he could choose his own path in life.

This did not take him long.

Sidney Dacre was a plucky young fellow, and thought that India would afford the widest scope for his talents, which were not of the most brilliant order, as may be expected from his early training.

To India he therefore went, and managed to shake the "pagoda tree" to a pretty fair extent.

In 1837 he thought he was justified in taking to himself a wife, and of this union Jack, who was born in the year of Waterloo, was the only result.

Fifteen years later Sidney Dacre received the intelligence that his father and his two brothers had perished in a storm near Bantry Bay, where they had gone to assist as volunteers in repelling a supposed French invading party which it was anticipated would attempt to effect a landing there.

This untimely death of his three relatives left Sidney Dacre the heir to the baronetcy and estates; and although he had plantation after plantation in the Presidencies, he made up his mind that he would at once return to the old country.

He therefore placed his Indian plantations in the hands of one Alfred Morgan, a clerk, in whom he had always placed implicit confidence.

This man, by the way, had been the sole witness to his marriage with Jack's mother.

A month later, and Sir Sidney and Lady Dacre, with their son, set sail in the good ship *Hydaspes* on their way to England.

Nothing of any importance occurred on the voyage, and the *Hydaspes* was within sight of the white cliffs of old Albion when a storm came on, and almost within gunshot of home the brave old ship which had weathered many a storm went to pieces.

All that were saved out of passengers and crew were two souls.

One, our hero Jack Dacre, afterwards to become the notorious Spring-Heeled Jack; the other, a common sailor, Ned Chump, a man who is destined to play a not unimportant part in this history, even if the part he had already played did not entitle him to mention in our columns.

And when we tell our readers that had it not been for the friendly office of Ned Chump our hero must inevitably have perished with the rest, we think they will agree that they owe the jolly sailor a certain amount of gratitude.

Ned Chump had taken very great interest in our hero on the voyage home.

Jack was such a handsome, bright-looking lad, that everyone seemed to take to him at first sight.

Ned's devotion to him more resembled that of a faithful mastiff to his master than any other simile that we can call to mind.

When Ned saw that the fate of the *Hydaspes* was inevitable he made up his mind that Master Jack and he should be saved if there was any possibility of such a thing.

The jolly tar bound Jack Dacre fast to a hen coop, and then attached his belt to it with a leather thong.

This done Ned threw the lad, the coop, and himself into the sea, and beating out bravely managed to get clear of the ship as she went down head first.

Had he not have done this they must inevitably have been drawn into the vortex caused by the sinking ship.

Fortunately for both of them Jack had become unconscious, or it is not likely that he would have deserted his father and mother, even at this critical juncture.

However, the *Hydaspes* and all on board, including Sir Sidney and Lady Dacre, had gone to the bottom of the sea ere Jack recovered consciousness and found himself on the shore of Kent, with his faithful companion in adversity bending over him with loving care.

As soon as Jack Dacre was sufficiently recovered, Ned proceeded to "take his bearings" as he expressed it, and knowing that Jack's ancestral home was somewhere in the county of Sussex, he suggested that they should move in a westerly direction until they should find some native of the soil who could inform them of the locality they were in.

They found upon inquiry that they had been cast ashore at a little village called Worth, in the neighbourhood of Sandwich, and that the good ship *Hydaspes* had fallen a victim to the insatiable voracity of the Goodwin Sands.

Shipwrecked mariners are always well treated in England, the old stories of wreckers and their doings notwithstanding, and Jack Dacre and the trusty Ned Chump had little difficulty in making their way to Dacre Hall in Sussex, though neither had sixpence in his pocket, so sudden had their departure from the wrecked ship been.

When Jack arrived at the home of his forefathers he found one Michael Dacre, who informed our hero that he was his father's first cousin, in possession.

"Yes, my lad," went on Michael Dacre, in a particularly unpleasant manner, "Sir Sidney's cousin; and failing his lawful issue I am the heir to Dacre Hall and the baronetcy."

"Failing his lawful issue!" cried Jack, with all the impetuosity of youth. "Am I not my father's only son, and therefore heir to the family honours and estates?"

"Softly, young man—softly," cringed Michael, "I do not want to anger you. Of course you have the proof with you that your father and mother were married, and that you are the issue of that union?"

"Proof!" cried Jack, fairly losing his temper. "Do you think one swims ashore from a doomed ship with his family archives tied round his waist?"

"There—there, my boy," said the wily Michael, "don't lose your temper; for you must see that it would have been better for you if you had have taken the precaution to have brought the papers with you."

"But," said Jack, quite non-plussed by his cousin's coolness, "Ned Chump, here, knows who I am, and that everything is straight and above board."

"Yes, yes, my boy," replied Michael; "and pray how long has Mr. Chump, as I think you call him, known you? Was he present at your father's marriage? I do not suppose he was present at your birth," and Michael Dacre concluded his speech with a quiet but diabolical chuckle.

"I have known him ever since the day we left India—" began the lad.

But Michael interrupted him by saying, in a somewhat harsher tone than he had used before—

"That is equal to not knowing you at all. I am an acknowledged Dacre, and until you can prove your right to that name I shall remain in possession of Dacre Hall; for the honour of my family I could not do otherwise."

"But what am I? Where am I to go? What am I to do?" stammered Jack.

Meanwhile, Ned Chump looked on with kindling eyes, and a fierce light in his face that boded ill for Michael Dacre should it come to blows between them.

Michael caught the look, and felt that perhaps it would be better to temporise, he therefore said—

"Oh! Dacre Hall is large enough for us all. While I am making the necessary enquiries in India, you and this common sailor here can knock about the place. It will, perhaps, be quite as well that I have you under my eye, so that if you turn out to be an impostor you may be punished as you deserve."

After a short consultation, Jack and Ned Chump made up their mind that it would be best to accept the churlish offer.

"After all," said Ned, "you know that you are the rightful heir. And when the proofs come over from India you will easily be able to claim your own."

"Yes, Ned, I suppose we had better remain on the spot."

"Of course we had," said Ned. "There is only one thing against it, and that is that if I ever saw murder in anyone's eye it was in your cousin's just now. But never mind, lad, we'll stick together, and we shall circumvent the old villain, never you fear."

So it was arranged, and Ned Chump and Jack Dacre soon seemed to have become part and parcel of the establishment at Dacre Hall.

The sailor's ready ingenuity and willingness to oblige made him rapidly a great favourite among the servants and employés generally, while Jack's sunny face, and flow of anecdote about the strange places he had been in and the strange sights he had seen, rendered him a decided acquisition to what was, under the circumstances, a somewhat sombre household.

So time passed on, and the first reply was received from India.

This reply came from Alfred Morgan, the late Sir Sidney's trusted representative.

This letter destroyed in an instant any hope, if such ever existed, in Michael Dacre's breast that Jack might be an impostor.

But there was one gleam of hope in the cautiously-worded postscript to the letter.

"Do not mention this to anyone. I am on my way to England, and I may identify the boy and produce the necessary papers—or I may not. It will depend a great deal upon the first interview I have with you; and that interview must take place before I see the boy."

"What did this mean?" thought Michael Dacre. "Did it mean that here was a tool ready to his hand, who would swear away his cousin's birthright?"

Time alone would show.

Then again the improbability of such a thing occurring would sweep over him with tenfold force, and he decided to take time by the fore-lock and remove Jack from his path.

Michael Dacre had not the pluck to do this fell deed himself, but he had more than one tool at hand who would fulfil his foul bidding for a price.

The man he chose on this occasion was one Black Ralph, a ruffian who had been everything by turns, but nothing long.

He was strongly suspected of obtaining his living at the time of which we are writing by poaching, but nothing had ever been proved against him.

In the days when Jack's grandfather had been alive, Michael Dacre, who acted as steward and agent on the estate, always pooh-poohed any suggestion of the kind, and sent the complaining gamekeepers away, literally "with a flea in their ears."

The arrangement was soon made between Michael Dacre and Black Ralph.

The former was to admit the latter to the house, and he was to ransack the plate pantry, taking sufficient to repay him for his trouble.

He was then to pass to Jack's bedroom, which Michael pointed out, and to settle him at once.

He was then to proceed to Newhaven, where a lugger was to be in waiting, and so make his way with his booty over to France.

This the cousin thought would make all secure.

But he had reckoned without his host.

Or shall we say his guest, as it was in that light that he regarded the real Sir John Dacre?

The lad was a light sleeper, and on the night planned for the attack he became aware of the presence of Black Ralph in his chamber almost as soon as the would-be assassin had entered it.

Brave though Jack was, he felt a thrill of terror run through him as he thought of his utterly helpless condition, for Ned Chump had been sent on some cunningly-contrived errand to keep him out of the way, and he had not yet returned.

That murder was the object of the midnight intruder Jack Dacre never doubted.

There was but one way out of it, and that was to rush up into the bell tower which communicated with a staircase abutting on his chamber.

Once here he could ring the bell, if he could only keep his assailant at bay.

At the worst, he could but jump into the moat below, and stand a chance of saving his life.

In an instant he had left his bed, and dashed for the door.

But the assassin was upon him.

Jack just managed to bound up the stairs, and enter the tower.

Ere he could seize the bell-rope he felt Black Ralph's hot

breath upon his neck. In an instant the lad had sprang upon the parapet. Then an instant later he was speeding on his way to the moat below, having made the terrible leap with a grace and daring which he never afterwards eclipsed, even when assisted by the mechanical appliances which he used in the adventures we are about to describe in his assumed character of Spring-Heeled Jack.

Our hero suffered nothing from his perilous jump worse than a ducking.

And it is very probable that this did him more good than harm, as it served to restore his somewhat scattered thoughts.

By the time Jack Dacre had managed to clamber out of the moat, Black Ralph had put a considerable distance between himself and Dacre Hall.

He had got his share of the booty, and whether Master Jack survived the fall or not mattered little to him.

He could rely upon Michael Dacre's promise that the lugger should be waiting for him at Newhaven, and once in France he could soon find a melting-pot for his treasure, and live, for a time at least, a life of riotous extravagance.

When Jack reached the house he found the hall door open, and without fear he entered; bent upon going straight to his cousin's room and informing him of what had happened.

Before he could reach the corridor which contained the state bedroom in which Michael Dacre had ensconced himself, Jack heard a low—

"Hist!"

He turned round and saw Ned Chump beckoning to him and pointing to the flight of stairs that led to their common chamber, and from thence to the bell tower.

Our hero having perfect confidence in his sailor friend obeyed the signal.

When the two were safely seated in their bedroom, Ned said, eagerly—

"Tell me, boy, what has happened?"

In a very few words Jack told him.

"My eye!" ejaculated Ned with a low whistle, "that was a jump indeed."

Then he continued—

"But who was your assailant? Could you not see his face?"

"No; it was too dark," replied Jack; "but there was a something about his figure that seemed familiar to me."

"Yes, lad, there was," said honest Ned Chump. "I met the ruffian but now, making the best of his way to Newhaven, no doubt."

"Who was it?" asked the lad.

"Why that poaching scoundrel, Black Ralph," answered Ned; "and you may depend upon it that your worthy cousin has laid this plant to kill you, and so prevent any chance of a bother about the property."

"What had I better do?" asked Jack. "I will act entirely under your advice."

"Well, my boy," said Ned, "take no notice; let matters take their course. We are sure to find out something or other in the morning."

And the two firm friends carefully fastened their door and turned in to rest.

In the morning the alarm of the robbery was given, but neither Jack nor Ned uttered one word to indicate that they knew aught about it.

"How did you get in?" asked Michael Dacre, roughly, as he turned towards Chump.

The would-be baronet's rage at the appearance of Jack Dacre unharmed, although his plate-chest (as he chose to consider it) had been ransacked, knew no bounds.

But Ned had his answer ready.

"I thought the door was left open for me, sir," he said, "so I simply entered and bolted the door behind me, and made my way up to bed."

"This is indeed a mysterious affair," said Michael Dacre, "but I have reasons of my own for not letting the officers of justice know about this affair. I have my suspicions as to who the guilty party is, and I think, if all is kept quiet, I can see my way to recovering my lost plate."

"Your lost plate!" said Jack, contemptuously. "Say, rather, my lost plate."

"I thought that subject was to be tabooed between us until

Mr. Morgan arrives with the proofs of your identity, or imposture, as the case may be."

"Very well, sir," replied Jack; "so be it. But I cannot help thinking that Mr. Morgan ought to have arrived long before this."

However, in due course the long-looked for one arrived.

But instead of coming straight on to Dacre Hall, as one would have expected a trustworthy agent to have done, he took up his quarters at the Dacre Arms, and sent word to Michael Dacre that Mr. Alfred wanted to see hint on important business.

The message, of course, was a written one, as the people belonging to the inn would have thought it strange had an unknown man sent such a message to one so powerful as Michael Dacre was now making himself out to be.

In an hour's time the two men were seated over a bottle of brandy, discussing the position of affairs.

"And if I prove to the law's satisfaction—never mind about yours, for you know the truth—that the boy is illegitimate, what is to be my share?"

"A thousand pounds," said Michael.

"A thousand fiddlesticks," replied Morgan, grinding his teeth. "Without my aid you are a penniless beggar, kicked out of Dacre Hall; and with no profession to turn your hands to. Make it worth my while, and what are you? Why Sir Michael Dacre, the owner of this fine estate, and one of the most powerful landowners in this part of the county of Sussex. A thousand pounds—bah!"

The would-be owner of Dacre Hall looked aghast at Morgan's vehemence, and with an imploring gesture he placed his finger on his lip and pointed at the door.

Then under his breath he muttered—

"Five thousand, then?"

"No, not five thousand, nor yet ten thousand," said Morgan.

"Now look you here, Mr. Michael Dacre," he went on with a strong emphasis upon the prefix.

"Now look here—my only terms are these: You to take the Dacre estates in England, and I to have the Indian plantations. That's my ultimatum. Answer, 'yes' or 'no.'"

For an instant Michael Dacre hesitated, but he saw no hope in the cold grey eye of Alfred Morgan, and at last consented.

The two now separated, but met again the following day, when the necessary agreements were signed, and Mr. Alfred retired to Brighton to make his appearance two days later as Mr. Alfred Morgan, the Indian representative of the late Sir Sidney Dacre.

"My poor boy," he said, sympathetically, when he first met our hero. "My poor boy, this is a terrible blow for you."

"What do you mean?" asked Jack; "it was a terrible blow to me when my father and my mother went down in the *Hydaspes*—but Time, the great Healer, has softened that blow so that I should hardly feel it now, were it not for the doubts that my cousin here has cast upon my identity."

"Ah! of your identity there can be no doubt, poor boy," sighed Alfred Morgan; "and that's where lies the pity of it."

"How do you mean?" cried Jack, an angry flush mantling his handsome features.

"How do mean, poor boy?" went on the merciless scoundrel. "Why, the pity of it is that, although I know so well that you are the son of your father and mother, the law refuses to recognise you as such."

"And why?" yelled Jack, with a sudden and overwhelming outburst of fury.

"Because," meekly replied the villain, "your father and mother were never married."

"But," cried Jack, thoroughly taken aback by this assertion, "you were the witness to the marriage. I have heard my father say so scores of times."

"Aye, my poor lad; but your mother had a husband living at the time," and Mr. Alfred handed a bundle of papers to the family solicitor, who had not yet spoken, the whole conversation having taken place between Jack and Mr. Alfred Morgan.

A silence like that of the tomb fell upon the fell upon the occupants of the room as the lawyer examined the papers.

Ten minutes or a quarter of an hour passed, then, with a sigh, the kind-hearted solicitor turned to Jack and said, with tears in his—

"Alas, my lad; it is too true; you have no right to the name of Dacre."

Without a word Jack caught hold of Ned's hand, and, turning to his cousin, said, in a voice of thunder—

"There is some villainy here, which, please Heaven, I will yet unravel. Once already you have tried to murder my body, now you are trying to murder my mother's reputation; but as I escaped from the first plot by a clean pair of heels and a good spring from the bell tower, so on occasion I feel that I shall eventually conquer. Come, Ned, we will leave this, and make our plans for the future."

"Aye, Master Spring-Heels, make yourself scarce, or I will have you lashed and kicked from the door, you wretched impostor!"

"Yes, cousin, I will go," answered Jack, impressively; "and I will accept the name you have given me, as you say I have no right to any other. But, beware! false Sir Michael Dacre, the time will come, and that ere long, when the tortures of the damned shall be implanted in your heart by me—the wretched, despised outcast whom you have christened Spring-Heeled-Jack!"

PART II

AS our hero uttered these words Michael Dacre's cheek paled visibly.

And indeed there was good cause for his apparent fear.

Jack Dacre had thrown such an amount of expression into his words and gestures as seemed to render them truly prophetic.

At this moment Mr. Reece, the solicitor, advanced towards Jack and, holding out a well filled purse to him, said—

"Take this, my lad; it shall never be said that Sam Reece allowed the son of his old playmate, Sid Dacre, to be turned out of house and home without a penny in his pocket, legitimate or not."

Jack, responding to a nudge from Ned Chump, took the purse and said—

"Thank you, sir, for your kindness. That there is some villainy afloat I am convinced, but whether I eventually succeed in proving my claim or not this money shall be faithfully returned. Once more, thank you, sir, and good-bye."

With this Jack and Ned left the room. As soon as they had taken their departure the "baronet," as we must style him for a time, recovered his self-possession to a certain extent.

Turning to the solicitor, he said—

"How much was there in that purse, Mr. Reece? Of course I

cannot allow you to lose your money over the unfortunate whelp."

The lawyer, who, although the documentary evidence was so plain, could not help thinking with Jack Dacre that some villainy was afloat, answered the baronet very shortly.

"What I gave the lad, I gave him out of pure good feeling, I want no repayment from anyone. And, mark my words, Sir Michael Dacre, that boy will return my loan sooner or later, and if there is anything wrong about these papers I feel assured that he will carry out his threat with regard to yourself."

"What do you mean, insolent—" cried the baronet.

But ere he could finish the sentence, Mr. Reece calmly said—

"You do not suppose that the matter will drop here? The poor lad has no friends, and I was stupid in not having detained him when he proposed to leave this house. However, I missed that opportunity of questioning him as to his life in India, and the relations that existed between his father and his mother. One thing is certain, however, and that is he will appear here again."

"Well, and if he does!" asked the angry baronet.

"Well, and if he does he will find a firm friend in Sam Reece," answered the lawyer. "I shall retain these papers— not by virtue of any legal right that I can claim to possess. So, if you want them, you have only to apply to the courts of law to recover possession of them."

"Then you shall do no more business for me," cried Michael Dacre.

"I should have thought," replied the solicitor, "that my few words had effectually severed all business relations between us. As it appears that you do not take this view, allow me to say that all the gold in the Indies would not tempt me to act as your legal adviser for another hour. A man who can behave to an unfortunate boy-cousin in the manner you have behaved to Jack Dacre, legitimate or not, can hold no business communications with Sam Reece."

"But how about my papers?" quoth the now half-frightened baronet.

"I will send you your bill, and on receipt of a cheque for my costs I will return you all the papers of yours that I hold—save and except, mark you, those relating to the marriage of the late baronet and the birth and baptism of his son."

The new baronet looked at his ally, Mr. Alfred Morgan, but saw very little that was consoling in that worthy man's face.

He therefore accepted the position, and with as haughty a bow as he could possibly make under the circumstances, he allowed Mr. Reece to take his departure.

By this time Jack Dacre and Ned Chump were more than a mile away from the hall.

Ned, although far more experienced in the ways of the world than Jack Dacre, tacitly allowed the latter to take the lead of the "expedition," if such a word may be used.

Jack, boy as he was, was in no way deficient in common sense, so perhaps Ned was justified in accepting the youngster as his leader.

For some miles not a word escaped Jack Dacre's lips.

At last they arrived at the old-fashioned town of Arundel, and here Jack suddenly turned to his companion, and said—

"We'll stop here and rest, and think over what will be our best course to pursue."

"All serene, skipper," answered Ned, "I am quite content."

Jack gave a melancholy smile as he replied to the sailor's salutation—

"Oh! then you don't object to calling me your skipper, although you have heard that I am base born, and have no right to bear any name at all."

"Never fear, Master Jack—or Sir John, perhaps, I ought to say—there is some rascality at work, and I believe that that Mr. Alfred Morgan is at the bottom of it. But we shall circumvent the villains, I am sure, never fear."

"Yes," replied Jack, "I think we shall."

"Ah!" said Ned, "but how?"

"I have not been idle during our long walk," said Jack, as the two entered the hospitable portals of the Bridge House Hotel.

"I have not been idle, and if we can get a private room we will talk the matter over, and see how much money the good lawyer was kind enough to give us."

"To give you, you mean," said Chump, with a chuckle. "It's precious little he'd have given me, I reckon."

They managed to obtain a private room, and over a plain but substantial repast they counted the contents of the lawyer's purse.

To the intense surprise of both, and to the extreme delight of Ned Chump, it was found to contain very little short of fifty guineas.

The sailor had never in the whole of his life had a chance of sharing in such a prize as this.

With Jack, of course, the thing was different.

In India he had been accustomed to see money thrown about by lavish hands.

Between the ideas of Ned Chump, the common sailor, and those of the son of the rich planter, there could hardly be anything in common as far as regarded the appreciation of wealth.

But, nevertheless, the friendship that had sprung up between them in so short a time, never faded until death, the great divider, stepped in and made all human friendship impossible.

As soon as Jack had satisfied himself as to the actual strength of their available capital, he turned to Ned Chump and said—

"This money will not last long, and I do not see how I can do anything in the way of working for a living, if I am ever to hope to prove my title to the Dacre baronetcy and estates."

"That's as it may be, skipper," said Ned, "but I don't quite see how we are to live without work when this here fifty pounds has gone."

"That's just the point I have been thinking over," said Jack. "I am not yet sixteen, but, thanks to my Oriental birth, I look more like twenty."

"That you do, skipper," chimed in Ned.

"Well, then, I'll tell you what I intend to do."

"Go on, sir," cried the anxious sailor.

"Some year or two ago I had for a tutor an old Moonshee, who had formerly been connected with a troop of conjurors—and you must have heard how clever the Indian conjurors are."

"Yes," replied Ned, "and I have seen for myself as well."

"Then," said Jack, "you will not be surprised at what I am going to tell you."

"Perhaps not, skipper—fire away," said Ned.

"Well, this Moonshee taught me the mechanism of a boot which one member of his band had constructed, and which boot enabled him to spring fifteen or twenty feet up in the air, and from thirty to forty feet in a horizontal direction."

"Lor!" was the only exclamation that the open-mouthed and open-eared sailor could make use of.

"Yes," continued our hero, "and I intend to invest a portion of this money in making a boot like it."

"Yes; but," stammered the half-bewildered sailor—"but when you have made it, of what use will it be to us, or, rather, how will it enable you to regain your rights?"

"I have formed my plan," answered Jack, "and it is this. I'll make the boot, and then startle the world with a novel highwayman. My cousin twitted me about my spring into the moat and my nimble heels. I'll hunt him down and keep him in a perpetual state of deadly torment, under the style and title of Spring-Heeled Jack."

"But," asked the sailor, "you will not turn thief?"

"I shall not call myself a thief," said Jack, proudly. "The world may dub me so if it likes. I shall take little but what belongs to me, I shall confine my depredations as much as possible to assisting my cousin in collecting my rents."

"Oh! I see," said Ned, only half-convinced.

The faithful tar had the sailor's natural respect for honesty, and did not quite like his "skipper's" plan for securing a livelihood.

But Jack, who had been brought up under the shadow of the East India Company, had not many scruples as to the course of life he had resolved to adopt.

To him pillage and robbery seemed to be the right of the well-born.

He had seen so much of this sort of thing amongst his father's friends and acquaintances that his moral sense was entirely warped.

So speciously did he put forth his arguments that Ned at last yielded.

The sailor simply stipulated that he should take no active part in any robbery.

For the faithful salt could find no other term for the operation.

To this Jack readily consented, and a compact was entered into between them as to what each was expected to do.

Ned promised faithfully to do all he could to assist his master in escaping, should he at any time be in danger of arrest.

Jack, on his part, promising Ned Chump a fair share of the plunder gained by Spring-Heeled Jack.

This arrangement entered into, the next thing was to make the spring boot.

Jack, who was possessed with an intelligence as well as physique far beyond his years, suggested that they should make their way to Southampton.

There, he argued, they could procure all they wanted without exciting suspicion.

Ned, of course, had no hesitation in falling in with this proposal.

A fortnight later and the boot was completed.

Completed, that is, so far as the actual manufacture was concerned.

Whether it would act or not remained to be seen.

To have tried its power in any ordinary house would have been absurdly ridiculous.

There was no place where it would be safe to make the trial spring save in the open air.

Jack had manufactured the boot strictly according to the old Moonshee's directions, but he could not tell to what length the mechanism might hurl him, and he was a great deal too sensible to attempt to ascertain the extent of its power in any enclosed space.

So one morning, Ned and Jack started off from the inn where they were staying, for a ramble in the country, taking the magic boot with them.

Ned had by this time managed to allay his scruples and went into the affair with as much spirit as did Jack himself.

In due course they reached a spot which Jack pronounced to be a suitable one for the important trial.

The spot was an old quarry, or rather chalk pit, where at one spot the soil had only been removed for a depth of about twelve feet.

Descending this pit Jack placed the boot on his foot.

Ned looked on in the utmost wonderment.

He could hardly conceive that it was possible such a simple contrivance should possess such magical attributes.

To his astonishment, however, he saw his young master, for as such Ned regarded Jack Dacre, suddenly rise in the air and settle down quietly on the upper land some twelve or fourteen feet above.

Ned, who, although a Protestant, if anything, had lived long enough amongst Catholics on board ship and elsewhere to have imbibed some of their customs, made the sign of the cross and ejaculated something that was meant for a prayer.

To his untutored mind the whole thing savoured strongly of sorcery.

An instant later and Jack Dacre, who had thus easily earned the right to be called Spring-Heeled Jack, had sprung down into the quarry again, and stood by the side of his faithful henchman.

"Well, skipper," cried Ned, "I've heard of mermaids and sea-serpents, and whales that have swallowed men without killing them, but this boot of yours bangs anything I have ever heard of, though you must know, it isn't all gospel that is preached in the forecastle."

"It's all right, Ned," said Jack, "and with this simple contrivance you will see that I shall spring myself into what I feel convinced is my lawful inheritance."

"I'm with you," said Ned, as keen in the affair now as Jack Dacre himself.

"I'm with you, and where shall we go now."

"Well, old friend, I must purchase one or two articles of disguise, and then I think we will make our way towards Dorking."

"To Dorking?" queried Ned. "I thought you would have made your way towards Dacre Hall, especially as you said you wished to assist your cousin to collect his rents. Ha! ha! ha!" and the jolly tar finished his sentence by bursting into an uncontrollable fit of laughter.

"Well, you see," replied Jack, "that's just where it is. Although my poor father never dreamed that he would inherit the family estates, he had sufficient pride of birth to keep me, his own son, in spite of all that they say, well posted in the geography of the entailed estates of the Dacres. I consequently know that more than one goodly farm in the neighborhood of Dorking belongs to me by right; and, therefore, to that place I mean to start to make my first rent collection, as I am determined to call my operations; for the terms robbery and thief are quite as repugnant to me as they are to you, Ned Chump."

"But, skipper, I never thought of you as a real thief," said Ned, "it was merely because I could not see how you could take that which belonged other people without robbery, that made me speak as I did. But if you are really only going to collect that which is your own, why there can be no harm in it, I am sure."

"That's right, Ned, and if I ever I do kick over the traces and make mistake, you may depend I'll do more good than harm with the money I capture, even if it should not be legally my own."

Four days later the two had arrived at Dorking.

Jack had provided himself with a most efficient disguise.

His tall and well-developed, although youthful, figure suited the tight-fitting garb of the theatrical Mephistopheles to a nicety.

Ned was perfectly enraptured at his appearance, and declared that he could not possibly fail to strike terror into the guilty breast of his cousin, the false baronet, should they ever meet again.

Jack merely laughed, and said that that was an event which would assuredly come to pass sooner or later.

It was an easy task, in a place like Dorking, to ascertain which were the lands that belonged to the Dacres.

The first farm that Jack chose as the one for his maiden rent collection was at a small place called Newdigate.

Jack chose this for his first attempt, partly because of the isolated situation of the farm, and partly because the tenant bore a very evil reputation in the neighbourhood.

Our hero, it must be remembered, was at that romantic period of life when youth is apt to consider it is its duty to become as far as possible the protector of virtue and the avenger of injustice.

It was currently reported that the tenant in question, whom we will call Farmer Brown (all names in this veracious chronicle it must be understood are assumed) had possessed himself of the lease in an unlawful manner.

It was also said that his niece, Selina Brown, who was the rightful owner of the farm, was kept a prisoner somewhere within the walls of the solitary farmhouse.

Rumour also added that she was a maniac.

To one of Jack's ardent and romantic temperament this story was, as our readers may easily conjecture, a great inducement for him to make his first venture a call at Brown's farm.

Ned received strict injunctions to remain at the inn where they had taken up their abode, and to be ready to admit our hero without a moment's delay upon his return.

The night was a truly splendid one.

As Jack set out on his errand, an errand which might as a result land him in goal, he felt not one tittle of fear.

"Thrice armed is he who has hit cause aright," runs the old saying, and Jack certainly believed that he was perfectly justified in the course he was pursuing.

Modern moralists would doubtless differ; but we must remember what his early training had been, and make excuses accordingly.

He arrived at Brown's Farm, Newdigate, in due course.

Now came the most critical point in the career of Spring-Heeled Jack.

This was his first venture.

Failure meant ruin—ruin pure and simple.

If his wonderful contrivance refused to act in the manner in which it had acted at the rehearsal, what would be the result?

There could be but one answer to that question.

Capture, ruin to all his plans, and the infinite shame of a public trial.

But our hero had well weighed the odds and was quite prepared to face them.

Arrived at the farm he had no difficulty in finding out the window of the room in which Mr. Brown usually slept.

This window had been so clearly described to him by the

Dorking people that there was no fear of Jack making a mistake.

With one spring he alighted on the broad, old-fashioned window-sill, and an instant later he had opened the casement.

The farmer was seated in a comfortable armchair in front of a large old-fashioned bureau.

He had evidently been counting his money and appropriating it in special portions for the payment perhaps of his landlord, his seed merchant, and so on.

The noise that Jack made as he opened the window caused the farmer to turn swiftly round.

Judge, if you can, his dismay when he found what kind of a visitor had made a call upon him.

On this, his first adventure in the garb of Spring-Heeled Jack, our hero had not called the aid of phosphorus into requisition.

His appearance, however, was well calculated to strike terror into the breast of any one.

Still more so, therefore, into the heart of one, who, like the farmer, was depriving his orphan niece of her legal rights, as well as of her liberty.

With a yell like that of a man in an epileptic fit, Farmer Brown sprang to his feet.

In another instant, however, he had sunk back again into his chair-rendered for the time hopelessly insane.

Jack, without any consideration of the amount which might or might not be due to the owner of the Dacre estates, calmly took possession of all the cash that he could find in the bureau, and then thought it was time to turn his attention to the alleged prisoner, Selina Brown.

Satisfying himself that the bureau contained no money save that which he had already secured, Jack was overjoyed at finding a document, hidden away in a corner of a pigeon hole.

This document bore upon it the superscription—"The last will and testament of Richard Brown, farmer."

In an instant our hero pieced together the story he had heard in Dorking, and arrived at the conclusion that the present Farmer Brown, although he had usurped his niece's position and concealed his brother's will, had at the same time, actuated by some strange fear, such as does occasionally possess criminals, dared not destroy the important document.

And here it was in Jack's hands.

There seemed no chance of immediate recovery by the farmer of his lost senses, so our hero coolly opened the document and read it through.

"As I thought," he muttered to himself.

"As I thought, the whole farm belongs to this girl, and this rascally uncle, one of the same kidney as my precious cousin, has simply swindled her out of her inheritance."

"However, I will see if I cannot manage to find her, and if I do, I think it will go hard if she does not recover her own again."

Then, taking up a pen, he selected a sheet of paper, and wrote upon it in bold characters—

> *Received of the tenant of Brown's Farm, Surrey, the sum of £120. And I hereby acknowledge that the above sum has been so received by me in payment of any rent now due for the said farm, or which may afterwards accrue until such sum is exhausted.*
>
> *(Signed) Spring-Heeled Jack.*
>
> *N.B.—If this receipt is shown to Sir Michael Dacre, as he calls himself, its validity will be accepted without question, otherwise let him beware.*

With a quiet chuckle Jack read this over to himself, then he laid it down in front of the jabbering lunatic, Farmer Brown.

"Now for the girl." Jack said, as he carefully put the will in one of the pockets of his capacious cloak.

The search for the girl did not take long.

The farmhouse was not a large one, and our hero's ears soon discovered a low moaning sound that evidently came from a garret which could only be approached by a rickety ladder.

In an instant Jack was at the top of the frail structure.

There, right in front of him, lay the object of his search.

She was a young and lovely girl about his own age.

Jack's heart gave one bound as he looked at her, then with a grateful sigh he said, fervently—

"Thank Heaven! I have come here. I take this as an augury that even if there is any wrong in the life I have chosen, I shall gain absolution for the evil by the good that will come out of it."

This philosophy was undoubtedly rather Jesuitical, but allowance must be made for the manner and place in which he had been brought up.

The girl seemed perfectly dazed when she saw Jack, but she betrayed not the slightest sign of fear.

She advanced towards our hero as far as a chain which was passed round her waist and fastened with a staple to the floor, would allow her, and with a child-like innocence, said—

"Ah! I know you, but I am not frightened at you. You have come to take me away from this. I do so long to see the green fields again. Take me away. I am not afraid of you."

For an instant and an instant only Jack hesitated.

His hesitation was only caused by his self inquiry as to what course he had better pursue under the circumstances.

He soon made up his mind, however.

With Jack to think was to act.

He had heard that one Squire Popham, a local justice of the peace, had expressed strong doubts as to the right of the present Farmer Brown to hold the farm.

To this worthy man's house our hero determined to convey the lovely child whom we have called by the unromantic name of Selina Brown.

To remove the chain from the girl's waist was work of no little difficulty, but perseverance, as it usually does, conquered in the end, and half an hour later Jack had carried the girl to Squire Popham's house, where, with a furious ring at the bell, he had left her, having first chalked on the door of the mansion the following words—

"This girl is the daughter of the late Farmer Brown, of Newdigate."

"Her father's will is in her pocket."

"Her wretched uncle is a jabbering idiot at the farm."

"See that the girl enjoys her rights, or dread the vengeance of 'SPRING-HEELED JACK.'"

In another instant, and before the hall-door had opened to admit the half-unconscious girl, Jack gave one bound and disappeared from sight, and so for the time ended the first adventure of Spring-Heeled Jack.

PART III

BEFORE we follow our hero any further on his extraordinary career we may as well finish the story of Farmer Brown and his niece.

When Squire Popham's footman opened the hall door he at first failed to see the girl so strangely rescued by Spring-Heeled Jack.

He, however, saw the chalk marks on the door, but was unable to read them—no extraordinary circumstance with a man of his class in the early part of the present century.

Then, turning round, he saw the poor girl.

There was a vacant look on her face that told the footman, untutored as he was, that she was "a button short," as he expressed it to himself.

The mysterious chalk marks and the "daft" girl were a little too much for the footman, and he hastened to call the butler.

This worthy could read, and as soon as he made his appearance, and had deciphered Jack's message, he directed his subordinate to call the squire.

When Mr. Popham, a typical country gentleman of the period, made his appearance, and read the inscription and saw the girl, his sympathies were immediately enlisted on her behalf.

"Confound Mr. Spring-Heeled Jack, whoever he may be, and his impudence, too!" cried the irate squire.

"Does he think that it requires threats to make an English magistrate see justice done?"

Then bidding the butler to call all the men servants together, he instructed the housekeeper to see after the welfare of the poor girl.

As soon as the men had assembled Mr. Popham read Spring-Heeled Jack's message to them, and then for the first time recollected that he had not secured the will.

He told one of the men to go to the housekeeper's room, and ask for the document which was in the girl's pocket.

During the man's brief absence the squire told the men what he intended doing, and that was to go over to Brown's farm, and, of the wording of the will proved Jack's tale was correct, to seize the unworthy uncle there and then, and clap him in the Dorking watch-house.

A hasty glance at the will soon informed Mr. Popham that Jack had not exaggerated the facts of the case.

"Now, my men," he said, "we will get over to Newgate at once. It is as I suspected. The present holder of Brown's farm has no more title to it than I have. Let us go and seize him at once. You have all been sworn in as constables, so we have the law entirely on our side."

We may inform our readers that this was commonly the case in those days, when the guardians of the peace we few and far between, and immeasurably inferior to our present police, both in intelligence and physique.

The journey took some three-quarters of an hour—a much longer time than had been occupied by our hero, in spite of the burden which he had to bear.

The squire ordered the butler to knock loudly at the door, and his commands were instantly obeyed.

After a brief interval—so short, in fact, that it proved that the inmates of the house were up and dressed in spite of the lateness of the hour—the door was opened by a frightened-looking old woman.

"Who is it! What do you want?" she asked.

"I am James Popham, one of his Majesty's justices of the peace, and I want to see your master. Where is he?"

"Please, sir, he is in his bedroom," answered the old woman. "He has had a fit, and has only just recovered. Hadn't you better wait till the morning?"

"What ho!" thundered the angry squire. "We come in the name of the law. Lead us to your master's chamber at once."

At this juncture a querulous voice somewhere in the distance was heard to ask what was the matter.

Mr. Popham answered the query in person, for, pushing the woman on one side, he hastily ascended the stairs, two steps at a time, until he came to the door of the room from which the voice had apparently come.

Throwing open the door, Mr. Popham strode into the room, followed by his men servants.

"Mr. Brown," said the squire, "I arrest you in the name of the king, for suppressing your brother's will, and keeping his daughter, your own niece, in captivity since that brother's death."

Farmer Brown literally shook with fear.

Jack's sudden appearance had temporarily turned his brain, and he had hardly recovered his senses when this new and terrible surprise awaited him.

"It is false," he faltered. "My brother left the farm to me."

"Then what about the girl!" asked the squire. "Even if your brother did leave the farm to you where is his daughter now? Produce her at once, or you may be put upon your trial for murder instead of the lighter offence with which I have charged you."

Mumbling a few indistinct words, and still trembling violently, the farmer led the way to the foot of the ladder leading to the room where his niece had been for so long a time imprisoned.

Here he paused, as if he did not care to go up the ladder himself.

"Go on," said the squire, sternly, "and bring the girl down without any further delay."

Very unwillingly, but compelled by the force of circumstances, the farmer made the ascent.

As he entered the room a loud yell of terror and astonishment burst from his lips.

"She's gone!" he cried; "that must have been the foul fiend himself who called on me tonight, and he has spirited the girl away with him."

"What do you mean?" asked the squire.

In a few words the thoroughly cowed and frightened farmer explained the occurrences of the night to the squire, winding up by giving a description of Spring-Heeled Jack's personal appearance.

"This is indeed strange," said Mr. Popham. "But if it will be any satisfaction to you I may tell you that your poor niece is safe at my house, and I have her father's will in my pocket. You are my prisoner, and my men will at once take you to the lock-up at Dorking."

The crest-fallen farmer could not frame an inquiry as to how his crimes had been brought to light, and in silence he allowed himself to be carried off to the watch house.

Farmer Brown was tried at the next assizes, found guilty, and sentenced to fourteen years' transportation, from which he never returned.

His niece through kind treatment eventually recovered her senses, and subsequently married and became the mother of a large family of children in the very farm-house where she had been imprisoned in solitude until the light of reason had fled.

When Sir Michael Dacre's agent called at the farm when the rent became due, he found Squire Popham's people in possession, for that worthy man was not one to do things by halves, and he had made up his mind that his own farm bailiff should look after the interests of the poor girl until such time as she might recover her reason.

The agent was shown the receipt that Jack had given for the money.

That worthy was immensely puzzled, but seeing that there

was nothing to be done save to take a copy of the receipt and return with it to Dacre Hall for further instructions, at once adopted that course.

When the baronet saw the receipt, and heard his agent's description of our hero—somewhat exaggerated as such things are apt to be by passing from mouth to mouth—his rage knew no bounds.

Of course he instantly recognised in the hero of the adventure his cousin, Jack Dacre.

Instantly summoning Mr. Morgan to his presence, for the unctuous agent had not yet returned to India, the two fellow-conspirators had a consultation as to what had better be done under the circumstances.

"My opinion," said Alfred Morgan, "is that you must grin and bear it. If you take any steps to secure the lad's apprehension and he is brought to trial, there is likely to be such a stir made over it as may bring witnesses over from the East, who may—mind you I do not say they will—but who may oust you from Dacre Hall, the title, and the other property which you possess.

"You must recollect that your late cousin was immensely popular in India, and his son would find a host of friends there to take up his cause."

The baronet had made many hasty exclamations during the delivery of this speech, but Mr. Morgan would not allow himself to be interrupted, and calmly continued to the end.

When he had finished, the baronet broke out rapidly—

"What do you intend to do, then? If the case is as you state, how do you intend to obtain possession of the plantations?"

"Oh! that's all right," coolly replied Morgan. "I care nothing for the barren honour of being called the owner of the Dacre plantations. I shall go back to India just as if I was acting for the rightful owner of the property—but with this important difference, that the rents and profits of the plantations will go into the pockets of Mr. Alfred Morgan."

"Then you won't help me to get rid of this spawn?"

"What time I am in England is entirely at your disposal," said Morgan; "but you must remember that my employer's interests require that I should return to India as soon as possible to look after his plantations."

And the wily villain concluded with a horrible chuckle.

"What course would you propose, then?" asked Sir Michael.

"Well, I think if I were in your place I would call on each tenant and warn him that some one is collecting your rents in a peculiar and perfectly unauthorised manner. Tell them the story of Spring-Heeled Jack at Brown's farm, but without disclosing your suspicions as to the identity of the depredator."

"Suspicions! Certainty, man," cried Sir Michael.

"Well, certainty, then," went on Morgan. "This will put them on their guard, and in the meantime you must wait and hope. If the boy continues this career much longer he is tolerably certain to get a stray bullet through his brains one of these days."

"I will start to-morrow," the baronet promptly said.

"And I will accompany you," said Alfred Morgan, with equal promptitude.

"Thank you, Morgan," replied Sir Michael. "I'll tell my man to go over to Arundel at once, and book two seats to London. We will go there first, as I have considerable property in the neighbourhood of Hammersmith."

"Have you?" sneered Morgan, with special emphasis on the pronoun.

The baronet coloured and bit his lip; but he dared not reply.

This was not the first time by many that his chains had galled him, and he heartily wished that Morgan were back again in India, although he knew that he should feel awfully lonely when the agent went away.

To return to our hero, whom we left as he was hurrying away from Squire Popham's house on the night of the rescue of Selina Brown.

Jack reached home in safety, and found the faithful Ned Chump waiting up for him.

The sailor's astonishment was as unbounded as his admiration when Jack gave him the history of the evening's adventures and showed him the money.

"£120!" said Ned. "My stars! and you haven't been away

three hours altogether. Why, we shall make our fortunes fast!"

"Ah! Ned, Ned, where are your conscientious scruples now? But, never fear, I do not want to get rich in this fashion. I merely want to obtain my own—and this, my maiden adventure, has been so successful that I feel certain I shall do so."

Ned, recollecting what he had said to our hero regarding the morality of their proposed course of life, looked rather sheepish, but he made no reply, and a little while later the two separated, and made their way to their respective couches.

In the morning Ned asked Jack what their next step was to be.

"I think we will go back to Arundel, and take up our quarters there for the present. From that place I shall be able to reconnoitre and find out what my precious cousin is about. And the very first opportunity that offers I will show him a sight that will raise the hair on his head."

"All right, sir," cheerfully replied the sailor.

PART IV

IN the comparatively short time that the two had been together, Ned Chump had had ample opportunity of finding out that he had enlisted under a captain who was pretty well sure to lead him ultimately to victory, and the tar had therefore fully made up his mind that under no circumstances would he attempt to question Jack's plans or schemes.

Arrived at Arundel, they took up their quarters at the Bridge House Hotel, and passed some time in comparative quietude.

Jack managed to keep himself well posted up in all relating to Dacre Hall and its usurping tenant.

This he was enabled to do by reason of a disguise which he had assumed.

No one would have recognised in the dashing young buck, apparently four or five and twenty years of age, the lad who had so lately been turned out of Dacre Hall as an illegitimate scion of the ancient house.

Ned had contrived to give himself something of the appearance of a gentleman's body servant or valet, and the two represented themselves to be a Mr. Turnbull, a young gentleman who had recently come into a fine property, and his servant, who had come down into Sussex to rest after a course of dissipation into which Mr. Turnbull had plunged on having come into his inheritance.

Jack, however, did not find out anything of importance for

some days, and then, quite by accident, he made a discovery which promised to make an interview between Spring-Heeled Jack and Sir Michael Dacre a very easy matter.

This discovery was made under the following circumstances.

Our hero was standing one evening in the entrance hall of the hotel, passing an occasional remark to the farmers and others who passed in and out, when he saw one of the gigs from the Hall drive up.

Jack was on the alert in a moment.

The man who had driven the gig was one of servants at Dacre Hall, who had shown a special liking for our hero, and this accidental encounter would give Jack an excellent opportunity of proving the strength or weakness of his disguise, even if nothing else came of it.

As the man descended from the gig and threw the reins to an attendant ostler, Jack advanced to the door of the hotel and met the servant from the Hall face to face.

The man looked at him full in the face, but not the slightest sign of recognition passed over his features.

Jack gave a quiet chuckle.

If this man who had shown him so many tokens of friendly feeling during his short sojourn at Dacre Hall failed to recognize him, surely he was perfectly safe from detection!

Not that Jack had anything to fear even if he was

identified, but he felt that with such an adversary as he had in the person of Sir Michael Dacre, his only chance of success was to meet his cousin with his own weapons, and so long as he could preserve his incognito the chances were greatly in his favour.

But this chance encounter led to much greater results than the mere testing of the strength of his disguise.

As the man entered the hotel Jack turned round and followed him to the bar.

"I want to book two seats to London by to-morrow's coach," said the man.

"All right," was the reply; "inside or out, the box seat is already taken."

"Oh, inside," replied the servant. "Sir Michael does not care about outside travelling at this time of the year."

"Oh, then, Sir Michael is going up to town, is he?" asked the attendant.

"Yes," was the answer, "and the gentleman from India is going with him."

"Rather a strange time for him to go to town, isn't it?" asked the hotel official, with the usual curiosity of his class.

"Well, yes, it is; but I fancy there is something wrong with his rent collector, and I think he is going up to take his London rents himself."

"Oh! I see," said the attendant as he handed over the receipt; "I suppose you'll take your usual pint of October?"

The man smacked his lips with an affirmative gesture, and the liquor having been drawn and consumed, remounted his gig and took his departure. As soon as the gig had been driven off Jack turned to the barman and said—

"If my man comes in, tell him I have gone along the river towards Pulborough, and ask him to follow me as I want him particularly."

"Yes, sir," said the obsequious attendant, and Jack strolled out of the hotel.

As soon as he had left the inn he turned into the park, and made his way to a secluded nook.

This was a spot which had been chosen as a meeting place for Ned Chump and our hero.

They were precluded from intercourse at the hotel, as it would have seemed singular for a gentleman and his servant—no matter how confidential the latter might be—to have held much private converse at a place like the Bridge House Hotel.

This spot had therefore been chosen, and it had been arranged that when Jack left word that he had gone towards Pulborough, Ned was to make the best of his way to the cosy corner of the park, where our hero awaited his advent.

When Ned made his appearance Jack plunged into the middle of the question at once.

"Which way does the London coach go?"

"Through Brighton, sir," said that worthy, "and then straight along the London-road."

"If we went post from here after she had started could we get to London before she did!"

"Lor, yes," said Ned; "why, we could give her three hours' good start, and then get to London first."

"That's what we'll do, Ned," went on Jack; "but say nothing about this until the coach has started. There will be plenty of time then to order the post-chaise, and there are some people going by the coach who might be suspicious if they heard of an intended trip to town."

"Yes, sir," replied Ned.

"Why, Ned, old fellow, have you no curiosity? I should have thought you would have been in a burning fever to know the meaning of this sudden change in my plans."

"So I am, sir."

"Then why not have asked? Surely you know I have every confidence in you?"

"Yes. I know that, skipper; and that's the very reason why I did not ask. I knew you would tell me all in good time."

"All right, Ned," said our hero.

And he proceeded to inform the sailor of what he had overheard in the bar of the hotel.

"So," he went on, "we'll get to London first, track them from the coach to whatever hotel or house they may put up at, then we will dodge their movements well."

"But what good will this do?" asked Ned, who did not quite see how his young master was to benefit by this.

"Why, don't you see? As soon as my unworthy cousin has collected the rents he is bound to take coach again, either for Arundel or to some other place where my property lies."

"Yes, sir?" queried Ned.

"Well, I intend to stop that coach, and make my rascally cousin hand over to me the proceeds of his rent audit, and I think that will prove a very good haul."

Ned, now thoroughly enlightened, grinned and wished our hero good luck in his enterprise.

The two now parted, and did not meet again until nightfall.

In the morning Sir Michael and Morgan made their appearance in due course, and Jack surveyed the departure of the coach from an upper window.

He met his cousin's eye more than once, but the latter utterly failed to recognise in the dashing young man about town the lad he had virtually kicked out of his ancestral hall.

Alfred Morgan, however, favoured Jack with a prolonged stare, and our hero more than once fancied he was recognised, but whatever suspicion might have existed in his mind was allayed when he asked the guard —

"Who is that young spark at yonder window?"

"He's a young fellow just come in for a lot of money, and mighty free he is with it too, sir, I can tell you," replied the guard.

"What's his name?" asked Morgan.

"Mr. Turnbull, sir," said the guard, as he proceeded to adjust his horn for the final blast.

This answer, so coolly given, speedily quenched any latent spark of suspicion that might have existed in the agent's subtle brain.

The coach started on her journey.

Two hours and a-half later Jack and his faithful henchman were bowling along at a rapid pace in the direction of London.

Arrived at Croydon, they inquired whether the Arundel coach had passed, and were informed that it had not.

The last stage of their journey was therefore performed at a slightly reduced pace, and the post-chaise arrived at the coaching-house fully half-an-hour before the arrival of Sir Michael and Morgan.

This enabled Jack to order a private room, which he desired might look out into the yard into which the coach would be driven.

The two were shown to a room which most admirably suited the purpose of our hero.

When the coach arrived there was Jack, snugly ensconced within a dozen feet of the top of the coach, but perfectly invisible to anyone outside, while himself able to see and hear everything. The coach arrived.

Jack had no difficulty in ascertaining his cousin's

destination in London; for, in an imperious voice, Sir Michael shouted—

"Get me a private coach at once, and tell the coachman to drive me to the Hummum's, Covent Garden, and look sharp about it."

This was his first visit to London since he had usurped the title, and he meant to make the most of his importance.

Bidding Ned follow, Jack swiftly descended the stairs, paid the score, and passed out into the streets.

Here he hailed a passing hackney coach, and arrived at the Hummum's some time before Sir Michael.

Jack engaged a couple of rooms, and then proceeded to make some slight changes in his disguise, so that Morgan might not recognise him as the man who had watched the departure of the Arundel coach that morning.

For the best part of a week Jack tracked his cousin with the persistency of a sleuth hound, until he felt convinced that the last batch of London rents was collected.

It was during this period that the supposed unearthly visitant first made his appearance in Hammersmith.

Although the newspapers of the time inform us that Jack committed many robberies, there is no doubt that this is incorrect.

All that he did was to visit each successive tenant after his cousin's departure, and ascertain from the terrified people how much money they had paid to the landlord.

PART V

THERE is no doubt that Jack caused an immense amount of harm by frightening servant-girls and children, and even people who ought to have known better; but we are not writing to justify Jack's conduct, but merely to extract as much from the diary or confession of Spring-Heeled Jack as will enable our readers to form some idea of what manner of man our hero was.

By these nocturnal visits on the Dacre tenants Jack soon found out how much money his cousin was likely to be taking home with him.

This sum was approximately £250.

A nice little haul for our hero if he could only land it.

During Jack's nightly absences the faithful Ned kept watch over the baronet and his friend.

One night on Jack's return Ned informed him that the baronet had sent the hotel boots to book two seats for the morrow's coach to Arundel.

"Then he is going straight home," said Jack. "Well, perhaps, it is better so. If he had been going further afield he might have banked the money. As it is, I know he will have it with him, and I'll stick him and the mail up somewhere in the neighbourhood of Horley, or I'll acknowledge that Michael is right, and my name is not Jack Dacre."

The following morning Jack ordered a postchaise to proceed to Horley.

From thence, after discharging one passenger, Jack, it was to take the other one on to Worth, and there to await until "Mr. Turnbull" made his appearance.

This programme was carried out to the letter.

Jack got out at Horley.

The carriage rattled on.

Jack took up his position at a fork in the roads, where he could see the stage coach some time before it would reach him, and at the same time be himself unseen.

In due course the coach came in sight.

Jack's heart beat nervously, but not with fear.

This was his first highway adventure, and who can wonder at his excitement!

In another instant the coach was upon him, and with a spring and a yell that threw the horses back upon their haunches, he rose in the air right over the top of the coach, passengers and all, shouting—

"Hand out your money and your jewellery—I am SPRING-HEELED JACK."

The coachman in his terror threw himself upon the ground, and hid his face in the dust, as if he thought he could insure his safety by that course.

The guard discharged his huge blunderbuss harmlessly in the air, thereby adding tenfold to the agony of fear from which the coach-load of passengers were without exception suffering.

Having performed this deed of bravery, the guard took to his heels and speedily disappeared from sight.

Jack's tall, well-built figure, dressed in its weird garb, was one that could not fail to strike terror into the breasts of the startled travellers.

One by one they threw their purses and other valuables at Jack's feet.

Our hero received the tribute as though he had been an emperor.

When the last passenger had deposited his valuables in front of Jack, that worthy youth said, with a sardonic laugh—

"Now you can all pick your money and jewellery up again, and return them to your pockets—all save Michael Dacre and Alfred Morgan."

In an instant the passengers sprang from the coach and collected their valuables, too utterly surprised by the turn events had taken to utter a word.

Sir Dacre looked at his confederate, and Morgan returned the look, but neither of them could force their lips to articulate a sound.

Jack stared steadily at his cousin through the two holes in his mask, and to the guilty man's fevered imagination they seemed to emit flashes of supernatural fire.

Pointing a long, claw-like finger at the would-be baronet, Jack said, in the most sepulchral tone he could assume—

"Beware, Michael Dacre; your cousin's last words to you

shall be brought home to you with full force. From this day forth until you render up possession of the title and estates you have usurped, you shall not know one hour's peace of mind by reason of the dread you will feel at the appearance of Spring-Heeled Jack."

"Who I am matters not to you. My powers are unlimited, I can appear and disappear when and where I will."

Then turning to Alfred Morgan, he said—

"Ungrateful servant of one of the kindest masters that ever lived, your fate shall be one of such nameless horror, that, could you but foresee what that fate would be, you would put an end to your wretched career of crime by your own hand."

Then gathering up the money and jewellery belonging to the two conspirators, Jack said—

"Good-day, friends. A pleasant journey to you. Just to prove to you that I can disappear when I like, look at me now."

In another second Jack had indeed disappeared, leaving behind him, as more than one of the bewildered passengers subsequently averred, a strong sulphurous odour.

The mystery of our hero's disappearance on this occasion is not difficult to explain.

While waiting for the coach he had discovered a convenient chalk pit— no rare occurrence in that part of the country—and into this he had sprung after uttering his parting words, which were of course intended for Sir Michael and Morgan.

After Jack's departure the panic-stricken passengers endeavoured to rouse the coachman from his prostrate position on the dusty road.

But for some time their efforts were vain, the man had fainted from sheer fright.

The guard, too, had totally disappeared. What were they to do?

At last one of the passengers volunteered to drive, and placing the still insensible driver inside, the coach proceeded on its way to its destination.

All the inmates of the coach looked askance at the baronet and his companion.

They looked upon these two as the Jonahs of the expedition, and it would probably have gone hard with both of them had anyone simply have suggested their expulsion.

Sir Michael was not slow to perceive this, and at the next halting place he resolved to leave the coach.

This resolution he communicated to Morgan.

"But," said the agent, "we have no money. How shall we get on so far away from home?"

"Oh! that's all right," replied Sir Michael. "I am well enough known about here—and even if I were not," he continued, in a whisper, "I'd risk everything to get rid of these cursed people who heard the fearful words that spectral-looking being uttered."

Morgan was about to reply, but a warning "Hush!" from the baronet stopped him in time, for more than one of the occupants of the coach seemed to be listening intently to the conversation between the confederates, although it was carried on in very low tones.

The guilty pair took their departure from the coach at Balcombe much to the satisfaction of their fellow travellers.

Sir Michael directed the landlord of the inn to show them into a private room.

The command was at once obeyed, for Sir Michael had not exaggerated when he informed Morgan that he was well known in that part of the country.

As Mr. Michael Dacre, the agent to the large and valuable Dacre estates, he had been well known.

As Sir Michael Dacre, the present owner of those said estates, he was of course much more widely known.

That is to say that people who would not have recognised the agent sought by every means in their power to scrape acquaintance with the baronet.

Once within the private room, and left alone with his companion in crime, the baronet breathed a sigh of relief.

"Phew!" he said, "I almost dreaded to enter this room, for fear that imp of darkness might have been here before me."

Morgan gave forth a nervous little laugh, as much as to say that he had no fears upon the subject, but he could not control his features, and if ever fright and cowardice were depicted on a human face, they might have been discerned on the not too prepossessing countenance of Mr. Alfred Morgan, the some-time agent to the Dacre Plantations in India.

"What is there to laugh at?" growled Sir Michael. "I have lost some £260, two rings, a gold repeater, and a bunch of seals."

Our readers will remember that gold watch chains were seldom worn in those days, the watch being usually attached to a piece of silk ribbon from which depended a bunch of seals. The time-keeper, a little smaller than one of the American clocks of the present day, was placed in a fob pocket, and the ribbon and seals depended on the outside of the waistcoat or breeches as the case may be.

"And I," answered the agent, "am in quite as sorry a plight, for I have lost £60, all the money I had left in England, besides my watch and chain."

This chain being a magnificent piece of oriental gold carving which Morgan had absolutely "stolen" from Jack's father, and consequently from Jack himself.

"Well," cried Sir Michael, testily, "it's no use crying over spilt milk; and still less use for us to quarrel. I will be your banker until you can draw upon your Indian property."

"None of your sneer, Sir Michael Dacre," began the agent, angrily.

"Tut, tut! man, let's make a truce of it, and if we cannot continue friends, let us at least avoid any resemblance to open hostilities."

"All right," sulkily assented Morgan.

"It is our only chance," went on Sir Michael. "I don't know who or what in the fiend's name this Spring-Heeled Jack may be, but I must confess that my nerves are terribly shaken by the events that have occurred since I turned my illegitimate cousin out of Dacre Hall."

"Illegitimate?" said Alfred Morgan with a sneer.

"That this so-called Spring-Heeled Jack," continued the baronet, ignoring the interruption, "is not an ordinary highwayman is self-evident, or he would not have returned some hundreds of pounds in money, and as much more in jewellery, to our fellow passengers by the Arundel coach."

"And it is also equally certain," said Morgan, "that this stalwart man who can spring over the top of a mail-coach, horses, driver, passengers and all, cannot be that puny lad who laid claim to the Dacre title and lands."

"Then who can it be?" cried Dacre, half in despair. "It cannot be that sailor, Clump, or whatever his name was."

"Chump, my dear Sir Michael, Ned Chump!" rejoined Morgan, who could hardly repress his sneering manner. "No, I do not see how it could possibly be the sailor; but one thing is certain—and that is that this individual is acting on behalf of your cousin, and although I have too much sense to believe in the supernatural, the whole thing passes all comprehension. First this Spring-Heeled Jack— and, recollect, your cousin adopted that name out of your own lips—appears at Dorking, puts a half-lunatic girl back in the possession of her property, collects more than the rent due to you from Brown's farm, but at the same time leaves a strangely worded receipt, which prevents you from doing anything but grin and bear it."

"True," broke in Sir Michael, angrily.

"Then we hear that a supernatural being has appeared to your Hammersmith tenants in turn, and has put to one and all the identical question—"

"How much rent have you paid to Michael Dacre?"

"True again," replied Dacre.

"You will notice," said Morgan, with what was meant to be cutting irony, "the absence of the 'Sir' in the formula."

"Yes, yes, proceed," snarled the unhappy wretch.

"Then we take the coach on our way to your ancestral halls—and what happens? Why this mysterious being about whom we have heard so much, and about whom we know so little, stopped our coach in a manner hitherto unheard of, half frightened the driver to death, takes all the money and valuables the coach contains, then calmly returns each of the other passengers their property, only retaining for his own use that which belongs to Sir Michael Dacre, the present head of that proud house, and that which belongs to Mr. Alfred Morgan, at your service, the agent for the Dacre plantations in the East Indies."

"Well, and what do you suggest, Morgan?" said the pseudo-baronet, growing pale as the agent went on with his cool and matter-of-fact statement.

"Well," answered Morgan; "I hardly know at present what

to suggest. To one thing, however, I have made up my mind."

"And that is?" queried Dacre, anxiously.

"To remain in England till this ghost is laid," replied Morgan.

The baronet gave a sigh of relief.

"Yes," the agent continued, "I am not going to run the risk of losing my hard-earned Indian estates—and that is what I feel sure I must ensue if I leave you to cope single-handed with the trio who are in league against you— maybe against me."

"Trio!" cried the baronet, faintly.

"Yes, trio! Jack Dacre, Ned Chump, and last, but not least, Spring-Heeled Jack."

To carry on our extraordinary story in a perfectly intelligible form it is necessary that we should leave the conspirators at the inn at Balcombe, and look out for our hero and his faithful comrade.

Jack, thanks to his ample cloak, had no difficulty in reaching the appointed place of meeting at Worth.

Ned Chump, who had been worrying himself into a state of nervous anxiety almost bordering upon madness, received our hero literally with open arms.

"How did you get on, sir?" asked the tar.

"Don't 'sir' me," replied Jack, banteringly.

"Well, then, skipper, if that will suit you."

"Oh, I got on prime, Ned," replied our hero, and he broke out into such a peal of laughter as astonished even Ned, who had already had many experiences of his young master's gaiety and exuberance of spirits.

Ned, as was his wont, remained silent, and Jack, who by this time perfectly understood his henchman's manner, went on to explain the events that had occurred since they had parted at Harley.

"And now," said Jack, "I will change myself into Mr. Turnbull again for a short time."

"Yes, skipper," said Ned, as he laid Jack's private clothes out for him.

"And then we will make for the Fox, at Balcombe, where the Arundel coach must have stopped after I had left it."

"Yes, sir," said Ned, in a matter-of-fact tone, as if his interest in the affair was a very minute one.

"If my surmise is correct," went on Jack, "Michael Dacre and the rascal Morgan will be resting there."

"Why so, skipper?" asked Ned.

"Because, after my word of warning, the passengers by the Arundel coach would not look with very favourable eyes upon those two arch conspirators, and I take it that they will have been only too glad to leave the coach at the first opportunity, and that must most undoubtedly be the Fox Inn."

"All right, skipper," replied the sailor. "I'm on."

By this time our hero had changed his clothes, or rather

had put those belonging to the supposed Mr. Turnbull on over his mephistophilean garb.

Some refreshments which had been previously ordered were now brought in, and after discussing these and settling the bill, Jack and his attendant left the house, the former telling the host that he might be back that way later on, but he was not quite sure, as if he met a friend of his at the Fox he might pass the night there, but, under any circumstances, he should return to Worth the following day, as his one object in coming there was to inspect the famous old church, the only object of general interest which the village possessed.

Jack had made this explanation as he did not want to carry his and Ned's luggage about with him on this reconnoitring expedition.

The landlord, only too pleased at the thought of seeing his liberal guest and his servant once again, gladly took charge of the travelling trunks, and Jack and Ned were soon far on their way toward a the Fox.

Entering the inn, Jack called for two flagons of ale, and in paying for the same took good care to expose the contents of his purse.

The host's eye caught a glimpse of the gold pieces it contained, and he instantly made up his mind that our hero should leave some if not all of them behind him.

"Fine day, sir," said mine host, by way of opening a conversation.

"Very," replied Jack, who wanted nothing better.

"Have you come down here to attend the coming of age of Squire Thornhill's eldest son?" asked the innkeeper.

"No," replied Jack. "My servant and myself are on a walking tour. We have left our luggage at Worth, and have merely strolled over here to see if my friend, Lord Amberly, is staying here or in the neighbourhood."

"No, sir," said the now obtrusively obsequious host, quite won over by "my friend, Lord Amberly," added to the sight of the gold in Jack's purse.

"Lord Amberly is not staying here; but we are not quite devoid of quality, for Sir Michael Dacre, one of our county magistrates, and a friend of his are at this moment inmates of my house."

"Sir Michael Dacre?" queried Jack, suppressing his excitement. "Why his hall is not more than twenty miles from here is it, how comes he to be staying at an inn so near his own home?"

"Twenty-five miles, sir," said the landlord, correctingly, "and the reason that he is staying here is that the Arundel coach was stuck up by a strange sort of highwayman."

"A strange sort of highwayman?" said Jack, in tones of well assumed surprise.

"Yes, sir, a strange sort of highwayman," replied the landlord.

And the worthy host proceeded to give Jack a highly embellished account of the attack upon the mail coach, adding—

"And as this strange joker, who calls himself Spring-

Heeled Jack, only robbed the baronet and his friend, the other passengers seemed to think as how they weren't much good, and so were glad to get rid of them, when they decided to stop here."

"And how do you know that they are any good?" asked Jack.

"Oh!" replied the loquacious landlord, "I knowed Sir Michael when he was the late baronet's agent—he's all right as far as I am concerned, whatever he may be to others."

"What do you mean?" said Jack, who had noticed something peculiar in the host's utterance of the last words.

"Oh! nothing, sir. Nothing!" replied the man, evidently discovering for the first time that his tongue had been wagging a little too fast.

Collecting his somewhat discomposed faculties as quickly as he could, the landlord put the question to Jack once more—

"Then you have not come here to see the grand doings at Thornhill Hall?"

"No," replied our hero, "I did not come with that purpose, but as my friend Lord Amberly is not here, I may as well stop until I hear from him, and in the meantime the Thornhill festivities will serve to prevent my getting the vapours. That is," he went on, "if you can accommodate my servant and myself with a bed."

"Yes, sir," said the landlord, with a bright twinkle in his

eye, as he thought of the contents of our hero's purse, to say nothing of the prestige that would attach to his house if only Lord Amberly should turn up to meet his young friend.

"Yes, sir," he said, "that is if you do not mind occupying a double-bedded room."

Then he continued in an apologetic manner—

"Sir Michael and his friend particularly stipulated for a double-bedded room sir, and indeed we have only one other in the house."

"Ha! afraid to sleep alone," said Jack to himself; "but I think I'll take a still further rise out of them to-night."

Then turning to the landlord, he said—

"Oh! a double bedded-room will suit me. We've been through too many adventures together to mind that, haven't we, Ned?"

"Yes, sir," replied the sailor with a suppressed chuckle.

With a fulsome bow the host ushered Jack and Ned to their apartments, indicating as he did so the one already occupied by the baronet and his friend.

Our hero ordered dinner for seven o'clock, and leaving Ned in the bedroom, proceeded down into the bar again.

Finishing his ale he strode out of the door and rapidly took in the geography of the house.

He had no difficulty in fixing the position of the baronet's room, and to his intense delight saw that the windows were mere frail casements of lead and glass, that hardly served to keep out the elements.

It was rapidly getting dusk, and re-entering the house Jack said to the landlord—

"I'm going for a little stroll, give my man all he wants, and put the charges down to me, and mind my dinner is ready at seven."

The host humbly bowed his acquiescence, and Jack again left the house.

He had about an hour in hand before dinner, and it was absolutely necessary for the success of his scheme that he should be back punctually to time, and he had a lot to do in that single hour.

To return to the would-be baronet and his fellow conspirator, who were still seated in the private room.

With Spring-Heeled Jack's name upon his lips—for that was the only topic of conversation between the guilty men—the baronet rose to ring the bell for lights.

Even as he did so a crash of glass was heard, and the object of their fears stood before them in the middle of the room.

"Strip yourselves, both of you," cried Jack in fearful accents, "strip yourselves to the skin. I told you I was ubiquitous—and I am here. Strip at once, or dread the dire vengeance of Spring-Heeled Jack!"

Too thoroughly frightened to ring the bell for assistance, Sir Michael and Morgan stood as if turned to stone, looking at the weird intruder into the privacy of their room.

Our hero found it difficult to restrain a smile, so ludicrous was the terror exhibited by his unworthy cousin and the agent.

But the faint ripple of enjoyment which passed over his face was not noticed by either of the conspirators.

Jack knew that he could not afford to waste a moment, even though the prolongation of his cousin's fright would have afforded him exquisite enjoyment.

"Strip yourselves," he therefore repeated, in still louder tones, "and quickly, too, or it will fare badly with both of you."

Sir Michael looked at his fellow conspirator, but, seeing nothing of an encouraging nature in his face, he commenced to take off his coat.

Morgan, accepting the inevitable, proceeded to follow the baronet's example.

Jack watched them closely, and every time one or the other of them paused he threatened them with horrible penalties if they dared delay any longer.

At last the two worthies stood in front of our hero as naked as they were when they first entered this world.

Bidding them roll their garments into a bundle Jack prepared to take his departure.

He unfastened what remained of the casement through

which he had so unceremoniously made his way into the apartment, and threw the broken frames wide open.

When the clothes had been made into a rather unwieldy-looking parcel, Jack caught hold of it, and, placing it on his shoulder, sprang literally over head and heels out of the window.

For some five minutes after Jack's departure neither of the naked men could move to call for assistance, so utterly cowed were they by the suddenness of the weird apparition's appearance.

Morgan was the first to recover anything like self-possession, and with an unearthly yell he sprang towards the bell-rope, and gave such frantic tugs at it that it very soon broke under his vigorous hand.

But he had succeeded in making noise enough to rouse the whole house, and a minute later the room was half-filled by the landlord and his servants and many of his customers.

"What is the matter, gentlemen?" asked Boniface.

"Matter, indeed!" cried Sir Michael, who had by this time somewhat recovered his normal faculties. "Matter enough I should think. That scoundrel who robbed the coach we came down by, has been here and has taken away all our clothes."

The titters and smiles that had been heard and seen among the domestics suddenly stopped.

Dim rumours had already reached Balcombe of the existence of Spring-Heeled Jack, and now here he was, or had just been, right in their midst.

A great terror seemed to have crept into the hearts of all of them, and none seemed inclined to stir.

"Someone of you rush after him," cried Dacre, angrily. "The bundle is a heavy one, and he cannot have got far with it."

But no one offered to start in pursuit.

"Confound it!" cried Morgan; "if one of you had had the sense to start off directly I summoned you the thief would have been caught by this time, or, at least, our clothes would have been recovered," he added, as the thought flashed through his brain that, perhaps, it would be well for his employer and himself if Jack were not caught.

"I don't think we could have done much good," said the landlord, rather nettled at the tone affairs were taking. "If this Spring-Heeled Jack, as you call him, is good enough to stick up and rob a coach-load of people, and is clever enough to come here and take the very clothes from off your backs, I don't quite see what chance I or any of my people would have against him even if one of us had started off immediately in pursuit."

The two sufferers, who had by this time entirely come to their senses, both immediately acknowledged that the landlord of the Fox was right.

Sir Michael, therefore, putting the best face on the matter that he could, said—

"True, landlord, true; and now, like a good fellow, see if you cannot get us some clothes, anything like a fit. Our present garb is not a pleasant one."

And indeed it was not, for Sir Michael was clothed toga-wise in a large tablecloth, which he had thrown over his shoulders in haste while Morgan was ringing the bell, and Morgan himself had only been able to secure the hearth-rug, with which he had enveloped his body, so as to preserve some semblance of decency.

Ordering the crowd of frightened servants and guests to leave the room, the landlord turned to Sir Michael, when they were alone, and said—

"I trust, Sir Michael, that you and your friend will leave my house as speedily as possible. I have my living to get, and this sort of thing is calculated to give a house a bad name."

"Insolent scoundrel—" began Dacre.

"No names, Sir Michael," answered the landlord. "I pay my rent and my brewers regularly. There has been no complaint made against the Fox since I have had it, and I do not fear anything that you can do to me. As to you yourself, the case is different."

"What do you mean?" angrily asked Dacre.

"What do I mean? Well, it is strange that this mysterious Spring-Heeled Jack should be always on your track. I have heard that he collected rents in your name at Dorking. Then you tell me that he robs you on the Arundel coach; and, by-the-bye, all the passengers by that coach put you down as the cause of the stoppage, and now you tell me that this mysterious being has entered your room by your window, some twenty feet from the ground, and, though you were two and he only one, he managed to strip and leave you as naked as you were when you were born."

Morgan nudged Dacre, and Jack's cousin had sense

enough to see that there was no good to come by continuing the argument.

"Very well," Dacre replied, in a gruff manner. "Let us have what clothes you have, and we will leave your house the first thing in the morning. It is too late to think of going on to Dacre Hall to-night."

The landlord acquiesced in a sullen manner, muttering—

"If Master Spring-Heeled Jack takes it into his head to return here before the morning out you shall both turn, no matter what the time or the weather may be."

With this Boniface left the room.

"This is getting serious," said Morgan, as soon as he was left alone with the baronet.

"Serious, indeed," said Dacre, testily. "I fully believe, Morgan, that the foul thing's threats will come true, and that he will make our lives a curse to us."

"What can we do in the matter?" asked Morgan. "Can you not suggest something? Recollect what you have gained by denying your cousin's legitimacy, and pull yourself together and let us see what had better be done, under the circumstances."

"Better be done, forsooth," said Sir Michael. "How can we arrange to do anything when we do not know whether our adversary is mortal or not. If he is mortal we dare not lock him up, as he evidently knows the secret of the Dacre succession; and if he is not mortal, of what I avail our struggles against him?"

"Not mortal, pshaw!" replied Morgan.

"The man's mortal enough, though there is something mysterious about him, I'll allow. We'll provide ourselves with a pair of pistols, and when next we are favoured by a visit we will test with half an ounce of lead whether Spring-Heeled Jack is mortal or not."

As the agent concluded, a wild, wailing shriek, ending in a peal of demoniacal laughter, struck upon their ears, and, rushing to the window, they beheld, standing on the top of the pump in front of the Inn, the awful figure of their hated foe.

With another unearthly scream Jack turned a somersault from the top of the pump, and long ere any of the inmates of the inn who had heard the taunting laugh had time to pass out of doors, Spring-Heeled Jack had disappeared, the gathering gloom leaving no trace behind.

Ten minutes later, and "Mr. Turnbull," looking as cool and calm as it is possible for a young English gentleman to look, returned to the Fox, and as he called for a glass of sherry and bitters he asked if his dinner was ready.

With a thousand apologies the landlord explained to him that, owing to the state of excitement into which the whole house had been thrown by the appearance of Spring—Heeled Jack, the dinner was not quite ready.

Jack, of course, asked for particulars, and the garrulous host gave the chief actor such a highly-embellished narrative of what had actually occurred, that our hero absolutely suffered in his endeavour to keep from laughing.

He succeeded, however, and bidding the landlord hasten

the dinner as much as possible, he entered the room reserved for himself and Ned Chump.

Here he found his faithful follower, and that jolly salt broke into a peal of uncontrollable laughter as Jack narrated the story of the last hour's adventure, winding up the tale by explaining that he had quietly dropped the bundle of clothes down a neighbouring disused well.

In the meantime a very dissimilar scene was being enacted in the room occupied by Sir Michael Dacre and Alfred Morgan.

Both of the conspirators felt dissatisfied.

Morgan inwardly accused Dacre of cowardice, and felt certain that eventually John Dacre would gain his own.

The usurping baronet, on the other hand, blamed Morgan for all the ills and evils that had arisen.

The two passed the night somehow, but it is comparatively certain that neither of them enjoyed even one half-hour's sleep.

Our hero and his henchman, on the contrary, partook of a capital dinner, smoked and drank and enjoyed themselves, and then slept the sleep of the just.

In the morning, much to the delight of the landlord of the Fox, Sir Michael Dacre and Alfred Morgan took their departure from the inn.

Our hero and Ned Chump, who had been informed that they were about to leave, had secured a position from which they could obtain a good view of the two disconsolate men.

And a pretty pair of beauties they looked.

Sir Michael was attired in a suit of clothes belonging to the landlord, and which was almost large enough to have accommodated his companion in crime as well as himself.

Morgan's borrowed suit fitted him a little better, but as the original owner occupied the position of ostler, gardener, and general factotum, it may easily be imagined that the garments were not particularly becoming.

"Well, skipper," cried Ned, as the post-chaise drove off, "no disrespect to you, but a more ugly, hang-dog fellow than your cousin I never saw; he looks well enough when he is dressed spick and span, but now he looks what he really is."

And Jack could not dissent, for it would have been difficult to find a more despicable-looking man than the mock baronet decked in the inn-keeper's clothes.

Jack thought it advisable to stop at the Fox for another night, and then sent over to Worth for the luggage.

"Not the slightest suspicion had been aroused in anyone's mind that this sedate Mr. Turnbull had had anything to do with the stoppage of the Arundel coach or the robbery of the clothes of the two guests at the Fox Inn."

Jack and Ned left a very pleasant impression behind them when they took their departure for Arundel.

PART VI

OUR hero had resolved to make the Bridge House his headquarters, as he had had such remarkable piece of luck there already.

For was it not owing to what he had heard while staying there that he was enabled to relieve his cousin and Mr. Alfred Morgan of their superfluous cash?

If our hero had known what important results his resolve to go back to the hotel at Arundel would have, he would have literally danced for joy.

This visit to Arundel led to an adventure which introduced him to his future wife, and we may safely say that hardly ever was man blessed with such a helpmate as was the wife of Spring-Heeled Jack.

The manner of our hero's introduction to his future wife was as follows.

The day after the arrival of Jack Dacre and Ned at the hotel a carriage drawn by four horses drove up to the inn door.

The occupants were an old gentleman and lady, apparently his wife; in addition there were two younger women, one might have been a servant or companion, the other was evidently the daughter of the old gentleman, so great was the likeness between the two.

Jack was lounging about in front of the hotel when the carriage drove up, and a strange but almost indescribable thrill passed through his whole body at the sight of the girl we have just alluded to.

People may laugh at love at first sight, but in the case of Jack Dacre it was an undoubted fact.

Our hero pressed forward to get a better view of the young lady who had made such a strange impression upon his ardent imagination, and as he did so he had the satisfaction of hearing the old gentleman say to the host that he intended to pass the night in the house if beds were available.

Mine host informed the traveller that there was plenty of room, and to Jack's intense delight the party entered the hotel.

"Hang it!" said Jack to himself, "she's a stunner, and no mistake. Now, how can I contrive to get an introduction to her? I wonder whether the old gentleman will go to sleep after dinner, and if she will go for a walk? I must keep my eyes open, and chance may befriend me."

And chance did indeed befriend Jack, for after the old gentleman and his family had dined, the young lady and her companion (for such the third female of the party turned out to be) started off for a walk.

Jack, affecting a nonchalance which he was far from feeling, sauntered out after them, keeping, however, at a respectful distance.

The two girls made their way down to the side of the river Arun, and choosing a quiet spot looked about for a seat.

A few yards further on they spied a tree, a large branch of

which stretched right across the towing-path till it reached nearly half way across the river.

Surely no more delightful seat could have been devised.

The two girls at once proceeded to take advantage of this charming resting-place.

Jack ensconced himself close by, just out of hearing, but where he could see every movement they made.

Once the two girls had made themselves comfortable a very animated conversation seemed to commence between them; then suddenly, whether by accident or design Jack did not at the time know, the companion placed her hand on the young lady's shoulder, and an instant later the only girl who had ever found her way to Jack's heart was being rapidly carried towards the sea in the swirling waters of the Arun.

Without waiting to see what became of the girl who had caused the catastrophe, Jack threw off his coat and sprang into the water.

Strong and steady was his stroke, and the girl had only just come to the surface for the first time when our hero was beside her.

One minute later and she was on shore, and Jack had the supreme satisfaction of seeing the rich glowing tint of life return to her pallid cheeks.

She opened her eyes and stared at Jack in wonder.

"Where is my maid, Ellen Clarke?" she asked, as she glanced hastily around.

"I don't know," answered Jack. "I was so anxious to be of service to you that I did not see what became of her. And, what is more, I don't think you need care much, for it certainly seemed to me that but for her you would not have been subjected to such a ducking. But come, let me carry you to the hotel. The sooner you get out of those wet clothes the better."

And without waiting for a reply Jack caught her in his arms and started off towards the hotel with her at a gentle trot.

To his sturdy young frame such a burden counted next to nothing.

Jack could see by the look half of terror and half of curiosity in her face that there was something to be accounted for in the manner in which she had fallen into the river; but he wisely refrained from worrying her with any questions at the moment.

Before Jack reached the hotel with his fair burden they met the maid, accompanied by three or four of the hotel attendants, making their way towards the river.

The maid's face flushed crimson, and then as suddenly paled, as she caught sight of Jack and her young mistress.

Our hero's quick, shrewd glance marked her manner, and he had no need to ask any question.

Whatever might have been her motive, beyond all doubt the companion had pushed her mistress into the river.

Young Dacre had gone through so much since his inopportune arrival in England that he had acquired an amount of worldly wisdom far beyond his years.

He, therefore, wisely held his tongue, and did not tell the girl that he had seen the "accident" and its cause.

The companion recovered her self-composure in a moment when she found that Jack did not accuse her of attempting to murder her mistress.

"Oh! Miss Lucy," she cried, "thank Heaven you are saved. I should never have forgiven myself had you been drowned. It was my fault that you fell in. I must have leant too heavily on your shoulder, and caused you to lose your balance."

These last few words were accompanied by a swift, sly glance at our hero.

Although Jack caught the look he took no notice of it, but simply strode on towards the Bridge House.

Surrendering his charge to her father, he proceeded upstairs to change his clothes.

While so engaged a knock was heard at the door, and a waiter handed in a card on which was written—

"Major-General Sir Charles Grahame will be pleased to see the saviour of his child at the earliest opportunity."

Our hero with a bright smile told the man that he would wait upon the general immediately, and he was vain enough to take a little extra care over brushing his hair, and so on, in case he should have the felicity of seeing the lovely girl whom he had just rescued from a watery grave.

Finding his way to the general's room, Jack's courage nearly deserted him.

He who had shown so much daring in endeavouring to checkmate his rascally cousin, felt as nervous as a young girl at her first ball, at the idea of meeting the lovely creature who had made such an impression upon him.

But his nervousness was entirely unnecessary, for on entering the room he found it tenanted by the general and a lady who was certainly some dozen years older than the charming girl he hoped and yet feared to see.

"Permit me to present to you my wife, Lady Grahame, Mr.—," said the general with a pause.

"Turnbull, sir, Jack Turnbull, at your service," replied our hero with a guilty blush, for he absolutely hated himself at that moment for the deception, innocent as it was, that he was practising on the father of the girl with whom he had so madly and so unaccountably fallen in love.

The formality of introduction having been gone through, the general, who had noticed the flush on Jack's cheek, but who had attributed it to a far different cause, endeavoured to place Jack entirely at his ease.

Thanking our hero cordially, but not fulsomely, for having saved his daughter's life, the general wound up by saying—

"But Lucy shall thank you herself in the morning."

"Then she is in no danger?" asked Jack.

"Oh! dear no," replied the general. "The doctor has seen her, and he says that it wants nothing but a good night's rest to put her right."

The lady had not spoken until now, having merely curtseyed when Jack was presented to her, but now she seemed compelled to say something, and, smiling in a manner that caused our hero to shudder, she said—

"Oh! yes, my dear daughter shall thank you herself in the morning, Mr. Turnbull."

"Your daughter?" said Jack, in accents of surprise, for the general's wife could not, by any possibility, have been the mother of the fair girl he had saved.

"Well, my stepdaughter," she said, with a self-satisfied smirk, for she took Jack's exclamation of surprise as a compliment.

After a few more words our hero returned to his own room, and gave Ned an account of his adventure, winding up the story by saying—

"And I cannot help thinking that Lady Grahame and the companion have leagued together to destroy that lovely girl's life."

"Monstrous!" cried Ned.

"Yes; monstrous, indeed. But I will spoil their little game. I shall keep close watch upon them, and if I find them in conversation together to-night I will treat them to a view of Spring-Heeled Jack, and in their terror find an opportunity of extracting a confession from one or both of them."

Our hero speedily changed his attire for his demoniacal garb, and, wrapping himself in his huge cloak, he passed down the stairs, and left the hotel without attracting any undue attention.

It was now quite dark, and, making his way round to the back of the house, where the general's suite of rooms was situated, Jack with one spring landed in the balcony which ran round that side of the house.

He looked in at the first window he came to, and the only occupant of the room was the old general, who was taking an after-dinner nap.

The next room he passed he did not look through the window. Something subtle seemed to tell him that this was where his loved one lay at rest.

But at the next window he paused and listened.

The words that fell upon his ears literally burnt themselves into his brain.

"Heavens!" he cried; "I am only just in time."

Another instant, and the occupants of the room, Lady Grahame and Ellen Clarke, beheld standing before them the terrible figure of Spring-Heeled Jack.

"HA! ha!" cried Jack, "your intended crime is such a monstrous one, that even I, Spring—Heeled Jack, fiend though I may be, am bound to prevent its consummation."

Only one of the two women heard these words, for Ellen Clarke had fainted at the appearance of the fearful apparition.

Lady Grahame was possessed of stronger nerves, or she would never have been able to plan the death of her lovely and innocent step-daughter.

For that was the purport of the conversation which Jack had overheard whilst standing outside the window.

It appeared that the whole of General Grahame's private fortune must pass, by the provisions of his father's will, to Lucy Grahame, but if she died before the general, then he would have absolute control over the property and could leave it to whomsoever he pleased.

Lady Grahame had argued to herself that if she could but remove Lucy from her path she could easily work upon the general to make a will in her sole favour.

This once accomplished how easy it would be to rid herself of her elderly husband, and with the wealth that would then be at her disposal she would easily be able to marry a younger and handsomer man, and spend the rest of her days in riotous luxury and dissipation—for such was the bent of her mind, and the general's quiet mode of life did not at all meet her views.

All this Jack had been able to gather whilst standing in the balcony before the window of Lady Grahame's chamber.

No wonder, then, that the sudden appearance of Jack in the midst of such a conversation should have sent the lady's maid into a fainting fit.

Upon the hardened Lady Grahame, however, his appearance produced no outward appearance of fear.

What amount of trepidation was at her heart Heaven alone could tell.

She stood erect and looked Jack dauntlessly in the face.

"I fear not fiend nor man," she cried; "the former I doubt the existence of, therefore you must be the latter. So name your price, Spring-Heeled Jack, I will pay it whatever it is, and trust to your honour to hold your tongue when you have received it."

Jack gave a demoniacal grin.

"Not that you could do me any harm by repeating the words that you have doubtless overheard," she went on.

Again Jack smiled his fearful smile.

"Who would take the word of a highwayman and midnight thief against that of Lady Grahame?" she cried, defiantly, now thoroughly convinced that she did stand in some amount of danger at the hands of this extraordinary being.

Jack made no reply, but seizing her by the wrist drew her towards the chamber door.

Vainly she struggled, Jack's powerful grasp bound her too fast for any chance of escape.

Surely but slowly she felt herself approaching the door that would lead her straight into the presence of her husband.

She was about to offer Jack money once more, though she felt certain from his manner that it would be of no avail, when the door suddenly opened and the general stood in the doorway.

With a startled look he took in the whole scene.

Ere he had time to inquire the meaning of the strange

drama being enacted before his very eyes Jack had released his hold upon Lady Grahame's wrist, and bowing gravely to the general, said—

"Pardon this intrusion, Sir Charles Grahame."

The baronet started slightly as he heard his name mentioned, but said nothing.

"Pardon this intrusion; but I am here on a very serious mission, and I must kindly ask you to answer any questions which I may put to you."

Again the baronet bowed, for he was strangely impressed by Jack's manner, and felt that our hero's presence in that room was caused by no sinister motive.

"Go on, mysterious being; whatever you may be, go on, and anything consistent with honour I will tell you."

"You have a daughter, Lucy?" said Jack.

"I have," answered Sir Charles.

"By the terms of your father's will she is entitled to the whole of your estates at your death, and you cannot alter it?"

"By the terms of the entail of the Grahame estate, which are bound to descend to the eldest daughter in the absence of male issue, Lucy is irrevocably entitled to my estates at my death; all that I have power over is any money which I may have saved."

The baronet answered freely and fully, for he was more than ever confident now that Jack was here for the good of himself and his daughter.

"If she died before you it would be in your power to dispose of the property as you chose?" asked Jack.

"Yes, for the entail would cease then. We two, my daughter and I, are the only living representatives of our branch of the Grahames, and the time-honoured baronetcy must die with me."

"Then let me tell you," cried Jack, rising to his full height and pointing his long claw-like finger at the still defiant, although silent, Lady Grahame. "Let me tell you that I have heard this night a plot—a plot so fiend-like that I cannot doubt but that you will feel incredulous at first, but a plot the existence of which you are bound eventually to believe."

"Go on, for Heaven's sake!" cried the baronet, hoarsely.

"At any rate," said Jack, "whether you believe my words or not I shall have the satisfaction of knowing that I have saved your lovely daughter's life; for after hearing what I am going to tell you, doubt it as you may, you will be put upon your guard, and that will be quite sufficient."

At the mention of his daughter's name the baronet gave a gasp, but he could not articulate the words he desired to.

Briefly but impressively Jack told the baronet how he had witnessed the attempted murder on the Arun, of course concealing his identity with Jack Turnbull.

Lady Grahame now for the first time spoke.

"Why listen to this midnight thief?" cried she.

"Silence!" thundered Jack.

Then turning to the baronet he explained that his suspicions being aroused he had listened outside the window, and he repeated word by word the conversation he had overheard between Lady Grahame and Ellen Clarke.

Horror, doubt, and uncertainty were expressed on the baronet's face as Lady Grahame vehemently denied the charge, showering every kind of vituperation upon the head of Spring-Heeled Jack.

Our hero stood motionless, the satanic grin on his face.

He knew full well that whether the old soldier believed his story or not, Lucy's life was at least safe from the machinations of her murderous stepmother.

Before the baronet had time to open his lips to reply to his wife, a fresh voice broke upon his ear.

The girl Ellen Clarke had recovered her senses, and had thrown herself upon her knees at the feet of the general.

"Oh! forgive me, Sir Charles," cried the girl, as she grovelled on the ground in front of the astonished baronet. "It is all true; but I was sorely tempted by Lady Grahame, who had me in her power, as I had once stolen a diamond ring belonging to her, and she threatened me with imprisonment if I did not comply with her request, or rather commands. Pray—pray forgive me."

The poor old man, who had faced the enemy on many a well-fought field, thoroughly broke down at this, and agonising sobs thrilled his manly chest.

Lady Grahame stood pale and silent.

She knew the game was up.

She had played her last card, and had lost.

Well, she must accept the inevitable.

She had not much fear of any earthly punishment for her meditated crime.

She knew full well that Sir Charles's keen sense of honour would never permit him to blazon his shame abroad.

For shame it would be for one who bore the honoured name of Grahame to stand at a criminal bar, charged with conspiracy and attempt to murder a step-daughter.

Jack surveyed the scene for a moment in silence.

Then he moved towards the window.

Turning to the baronet, he said—

"My work is done; I have saved your daughter's life; with the punishment you may mete out to these two wretched women I have nothing to do. Farewell!"

"Stay!" cried the baronet, recovering his self-possession, after a struggle. "Who are you, mysterious man? At least let me thank you for my child's life."

"I want no thanks," said Jack; "and as to who I am that I cannot at present tell, for there are reasons why my identity should be concealed. Some day, perhaps, I may present myself to you in proper person."

"But how shall I know that whoever presents himself to me is really yourself?" asked Sir Charles.

"Give me your signet ring," said Jack; "and rest assured that whoever hands it back to you will be Spring-Heeled Jack in person."

The general at once complied, and endeavoured to shake Jack by the hand, but our hero dexterously contrived to wrench it away just as he received the ring.

"No, Sir Charles," said he; "I cannot shake you or any honest man by the hand just now. A time may come—nay, it shall come—when I can do so. Till then, farewell!"

Another instant and Jack had left the room as suddenly as he had entered it.

We will leave the two guilty women and the baronet together for the present, and follow Jack.

Taking his cloak from the balcony, where he had placed it, our hero pulled it closely round him, and, with a spring, alighted on Mother Earth once more.

Hastening round to the front of the hotel, he ordered some brandy to be sent to his room, and calling to Ned, who was in one of the side bars, used as a tap, Jack proceeded to his own room.

Ned Chump followed immediately afterwards, and our hero soon put him in possession of the extraordinary event of the last hour.

"Well, Ned," said he, "I shall commence direct and final operations at once. I have just about time to reach Dacre Hall a couple of hours before daylight."

"Dacre Hall!" cried the astounded salt. "Why, does your honour recollect how far it is?"

"Yes, perfectly," was the reply.

Ned, seeing that his master had made up his mind thoroughly for the adventure, did not further attempt to dissuade him from it.

"I have reckoned the distance," then went on Jack, "and I have ample time to perform all that I intend to do long before the sun peeps above the horizon. Meanwhile give me a glass of that brandy which the waiter has just brought in, and put the rest in my flask. I shall probably have need of it ere my return. In case I am not back till late in the day, which might make my absence noticed, you had better tell the landlord in the morning that I am slightly indisposed, and you can order my meals to be brought to my room just as if I really was confined to my bed."

"But how about your return? How will you get in?"

"Ha! ha!" laughed Jack. "Why, Ned, you have only to leave the casement of the bedroom wide open, and when I come back surely I can vault on the sill, and so make my entry without being seen."

"Well, you are a wonder, skipper, you are a wonder. Talk about what's his name, Baron—-Baron—"

"Munchausen," put in our hero.

"Yes, skipper, that's the name, but I cannot pronounce it. But talk about he, why, nothing that he wrote about is half so wonderful as what you have already done, let alone what you are going to do."

"Well, good-bye for the present, Ned, I must be off now."

And shaking Ned warmly by the hand the sailor said—

"And may all good luck follow you."

Jack sprang lightly from the casement window, and a quarter of an hour later was considerably over a mile on his way to Dacre Hall, so rapid was the pace at which he was proceeding.

Ned's wondering admiration at his master's powers and good generalship was in no way misplaced, for even while the conversation just narrated was taking place Jack had packed the garments usually worn by Mr. Turnbull into a compact parcel which he attached by a hook to the lining of his capacious cloak.

This he had done because he knew that after his mission at Dacre Hall was performed some hours must elapse before he could regain his quarters at the Bridge House Hotel, Arundel.

By taking the plain clothes with him he could make everything safe.

All he had to do was to deposit the bundle in some convenient nook, and then, when his mission was accomplished, he could regain possession of the clothes, and, by placing them over his tight-fitting disguise, and removing his mask and other facial disfigurements, he could speedily transform himself from Spring-Heeled Jack into Jack Turnbull.

In the garb of that young gentleman, and with the cloak slung over his arm, he could go anywhere he pleased during the time which must elapse ere he could return to his hotel.

About a mile from Dacre Hall he met with the only adventure which befel him on his midnight journey.

He heard, apparently some little way in front of him, the sound of a horse's hoofs quietly ambling along the road.

Jack thought to himself—

"That's a farmer going to Lewes market, I'll be bound. Shall I give him a fright, or not?"

Our readers must recollect that Jack was young, and blessed with health and excellent spirits (or he could never have fought against fate as he did), so they will, undoubtedly, excuse the temptation which passed through his mind to frighten the approaching traveller, be he farmer or be he squire.

But ere he had made up his mind whether he should play one of his practical jokes or not, he heard a loud voice cry—

"Stand and deliver!"

This was by no means an uncommon cry in those days, but it was the first time that our hero had had the pleasure of beholding a real live highwayman, so he pushed rapidly along the road until a bend in it revealed a strange spectacle.

An apparently well-to-do farmer, on a smart and sleek-looking cob, was in the middle of the road.

At the side, where a retired lane branched off, stood what seemed to Jack one of the grandest sights he had ever beheld.

The sight in question was worthy of the pencil of Frith, whose picture of Claude Duval, the highwayman, dancing a coranto with a lady in Hounslow Heath, is doubtless well known to most of our readers.

One of the grandest thoroughbreds Jack had ever seen stood motionless at the mouth of the lane, from the ambuscade of which it had evidently just emerged.

Mounted on the back of this magnificent charger was a man who might have stood as model for the greatest sculptor the world ever produced.

His whole form, save his lips, was as motionless as that of the noble animal he bestrode.

His dress was picturesque in the extreme.

He had eschewed the orthodox scarlet, save that in his three-cornered hat he wore the bright red feather of a flamingo.

His tunic, however, was of a beautiful blue, relieved here and there with silver.

His white buckskin breeches, and his well-blacked boots, rising far above his knees, stood out sharply and well-defined in the cold glare of the moon.

His right arm was pointed straight at the head of the unhappy-looking farmer, and that right arm ended in a hand containing a handsomely mounted pistol.

"Good Mr. Highwayman, spare me! I have but little money about me, and that I am going to take over to my landlord's agent, who threatens to turn me out of my farm unless I pay him something by eight o'clock in the morning, and I have now only just got time to get to his house by that hour."

"Liar!" thundered the highwayman. "I know you are loaded with money, for you are off to Lewes market to buy cattle. Hand over your money, or you are a dead man."

Here was an opportunity for our hero's practical joke, too good to be resisted.

He grasped the situation in an instant, and ere the highwayman had time to fire his pistol, or the farmer to produce his cash, Spring-Heeled Jack, with an awful cry, sprang in the air clean over the heads of the highwayman and his destined victim.

It would be utterly impossible to find words to describe Jack's appearance as he went over the heads of the two horsemen.

The rapidity of his flight in the air distended the flaps of his coat, until they resembled a pair of wings.

His peculiar costume, fitting so tightly to his skin, made him look like a huge bat, with a body of brilliant scarlet.

With a yell of fear from the farmer, and a screech of unearthly sound from the animal he bestrode, horse and rider disappeared along the road to Lewes.

The highwayman on the other hand did not stir, and as well trained was his beautiful steed, that although it trembled with fear for an instant, it did not attempt to bolt as the farmer's horse had done.

As Jack touched the ground again the highwayman took aim at our hero and fired.

The part which he had intended to hit was Jack's forehead, and had the forehead have been where it was apparently situated, the bullet must have gone crashing straight through our hero's skull.

As it was, however, Jack's mask was so constructed as to make his face look about two inches longer than it really was.

This two inches of added matter formed the supposed cranium through which the highwayman's bullet had sped.

With another shriek more supernatural than the first Jack wheeled round, and sprang once more over his adversary's head.

This was too much even for the highwayman, who up till now had not known what fear was.

He had watched the track of his bullet clean through the uncanny-looking being's brain, and felt that it would be impossible to cope with an enemy possessing such extraordinary if not unearthly attributes.

Digging his spurs right up to the hilt in his steed's sides, he lifted the reins, and just as our hero gave a loud mocking laugh of defiance, and waved his plumed cap in the air, the highwayman gave his horse a cut, and leaping the hedge at the roadside, the noble steed and its rider were soon lost to view.

"Well, that was a lark," said Jack to himself as he rapidly strode on in the direction of Dacre Hall; "but it was a close shave, though, for I felt that bullet graze the top of my scalp in a most decidedly unpleasant manner."

Half-an-hour later, and he was at the lodge-gates of his ancestral home.

Everything now depended upon his caution, and Jack was resolved that no fault of his should mar the performance of his plans.

He knew the room which had been allotted to Morgan when he first took up his abode at the Hall, but still that room might have been changed, and it would have been fatal to our hero's scheme to have made a mistake on that score.

The only thing, therefore, was to rouse up the lodge-keeper, and find from him in his certain fright the position of the room occupied by Mr. Alfred Morgan.

The lodge consisted of only two rooms—one up and one downstairs.

In the former Jack knew that the lodge-keeper slept.

There was a stone ballustrade outside the window of the bedroom, and on to this Jack lightly sprang.

To open the casement was an easy task.

This done, Jack cried out, in sepulchral tones—

"Awake, awake, awake! old man, awake!"

The lodge-keeper woke with a start, but he was not so frightened as Jack had expected him to be.

The fact of the matter was, Michael Dacre was not at all popular with the servants, and they had heard with some amount of delight of the various adventures he and Morgan had had with Jack.

"Good Mr. Spring-Heeled Jack," cried the lodge-keeper, "what do you want? If it is anything I can do for you tell me, and consider it done."

"I merely want to know in which room Mr. Morgan sleeps," replied Jack, highly delighted at the turn things had taken.

"In the blue room, sir," answered the lodge-keeper.

"Can I trust you not to raise an alarm for an hour or so? I have important business with Mr. Alfred Morgan, but shall not trouble your master."

"Aye, Mr. Spring-Heeled Jack, that you can," he said; "and if you can only frighten him out of this place you will earn the thanks of the whole household."

The man's tone was so self-evidently sincere that Jack, with a farewell warning, sprang to the ground, and hastened towards the window of the blue room.

To his surprise and momentary annoyance, he found that there was no vestige of a sill to the window.

The diamond-paned leaden casement was flush with the outer wall.

After a brief consideration, Jack made up his mind.

"I'll risk it," he said. "I have been successful so far, and surely I shall not fail now."

In another instant he had sprang harlequin-like clean through the window, carrying before him glass, frame, and all.

As he dashed like a stone from a catapult into the room his head struck against a human form, and when our hero had recovered his lost balance he discovered in the full light of the moon Morgan lying prone on the floor.

"Rise, and give me all the papers you have, or stay—you can lay where you are. I can see your valise there, and there, I know, you carry your private journal, and so on. I'll take it, and save you the trouble of rising. Lay where you are, and don't attempt to leave this house for three hours, or fear the hangman, for yours is a hanging offence."

Without another word Jack flung the valise out of the window, and speedily followed it himself.

As Jack left the room Morgan rose from the floor, and, trembling with fear, said—

"Fear the hangman! Fear the hangman, indeed! I fear nothing but this cursed Spring-Heeled Jack, who seems to haunt every moment of my life. I'll end it at once."

And end it he did, for half-an-hour later the dead body of Alfred Morgan was swinging from a hook in a rafter above his bed.

He had cheated the hangman, but he had hanged himself.

Jack did not reach the Bridge House until late the next night, when all was quiet in the hotel.

He had no difficulty in effecting an entrance into the bedroom, but he found he could not carry the valise up with him, so he secreted it in an outhouse.

He rapidly made Ned acquainted with the events which had occurred, and wound up by saying—

"And I really believe that the valise contains the proofs of my cousin's and his accomplice's villainy."

And so it proved in the morning, when Ned, who had risen very early, had contrived to smuggle the bag in unseen.

There lay every link in the chain of fraud, including a paper signed by the baronet and witnessed by two of the hall servants, stating that he was well aware that Jack was legitimate and the rightful heir to the Dacre baronetcy and estates.

"I must see Sir Charles Grahame about this," said Jack.

"He has enquired for you several times during your absence, Sir John," replied the faithful fellow.

A glow of pride passed over Jack's face as he stretched forth his hand to Ned.

"Thanks, old fellow; it is only fitting that you, who have stuck to me in adversity, should be the first to congratulate me in my prosperity. Go and ask the general if he can favour me with an interview."

Ned immediately obeyed, and a quarter of an hour later our hero was closeted with Sir Charles Grahame. Little more remains to be told.

The general was delighted when he found that the man who had twice saved his daughter's life, first in the guise of Jack Turnbull, and secondly in that of Spring-Heeled Jack, should turn out to be no less a personage than Sir John Dacre, of Dacre Hall, Surrey.

In answer to an inquiry made by Jack, Sir Charles informed our hero that Lady Graham had consented, to avoid scandal, to become the inmate of a private lunatic asylum for not less than two years; if she behaved herself during that time Sir Charles intended to take steps for her liberation, and to provide her with an income which would enable her to live in comparative obscurity abroad.

Jack and the general ordered a chaise, and started at once for Dacre Hall, armed with Mr. Morgan's documents.

The task before them was an easier one than they had anticipated.

Michael Dacre had been so shocked by the suicide of Morgan that he at once caved in, and agreed to quit the country, Jack, of course, having no wish to prosecute any one of his own kith and kin, no matter how treacherous his conduct might have been.

In due course, as our readers must have guessed, Jack and Lucy were married.

Ned was appointed to a post of trust at the hall, and as children grew up around them few mortals enjoyed so much earthly happiness as the family and household of Sir John Dacre.

Our story is ended.

After Jack's resumption of his title many scamps and ruffians played the part of Spring-Heeled Jack in various garbs in and around London, but the story which we have told of brave Jack Dacre is the only authentic history of Spring-Heeled Jack.